EARLY PRAISE FOR
THE TURTLEDOVE'S SECRET

"THE SUPERLATIVE PEN OF LAURA HASTINGS
. . . IS AT ITS EXPLOSIVE BEST IN THIS RIVET-
ING NEW ROMANTIC THRILLER. . . . If you're
looking for a surefire escape from the everyday blahs, this
mesmerizing delight provides the perfect means to do so."
—*Romantic Times*

AND THE CRITICS LOVE . . .
Laura Hastings's previous novel of romantic suspense
THE NIGHTINGALE'S SECRET

"An engaging blend of mystery and romance."
—*Publishers Weekly*

"A SPELLBINDING NOVEL OF EXPLOSIVE IN-
TRIGUE AND NONSTOP EXCITEMENT . . . one of
this year's best novels of romantic suspense!"
—*Romantic Times*

"A feisty heroine, world-weary hero and enough tension
to satisfy the most intrepid reader of spy thrillers. Expect
the best from this author, she always comes through!"
—*Heartland Critiques*

HELD CAPTIVE BY
HISTORY'S DEEPEST MYSTERY

JOCELYN MERRIMAN: she had risen from lower-class origins to become New York's most prestigious antiques curator . . . when the greatest find of her career brings back the love of her hidden past.

RIORDAN NOLAN: an antiquities specialist who reads in a stolen scroll the secret of the ages . . . and discovers in an elegant woman the ardent girl he lost long ago.

BRENDAN NOLAN: a powerful priest and Riordan's twin brother, determined to retrieve the enigmatic document that could shake the foundations of his faith.

HASSAN SALEEM: despite survival skills honed in the cauldron of Middle East intrigues, he realizes too late the price he must pay for possession of the sacred scroll.

THE TURTLEDOVE'S SECRET

The TURTLEDOVE'S SECRET

LAURA HASTINGS

A DELL BOOK

FIC
PB

Published by
Dell Publishing
a division of
Bantam Doubleday Dell Publishing Group, Inc.
666 Fifth Avenue
New York, New York 10103

ISBN: 0-440-20834-3

Printed in the United States of America

Published simultaneously in Canada

June 1992

10 9 8 7 6 5 4 3 2 1

RAD

Rise up, my love, my fair one and come away
for, lo, the winter is past, the rain is over
   and gone;
the flowers appear on the earth;
the time of the singing of birds is come,
and the voice of the turtledove is heard in
   our land

           —Song of Solomon 2:10–12

1

It was one of those days when they should have closed New York, strung chains across the tunnels and bridges, and hung out signs that said "DANGER—UNFIT FOR HUMAN HABITATION." It would have been a kindness.

The air was thick enough to cut with a buzz saw, the sky was a torpid yellow gray, and the sidewalks stank from the two-week-long garbage collectors's strike. Even the usually cheerful Caribbean peddlers along Fifth Avenue looked as though they'd rather be knocking back papaya juice on a sleepy Antilles beach instead of standing where they were, trying to hawk fake Vuitton bags and the odd Rolex rip-off.

So would Jocelyn Merriman. She got off the bus at Seventy-second Street and headed for her office two blocks away, thinking that if she didn't breathe too deeply she'd make it. Maybe.

She had a headache, the kind she got behind her eyes every time she slept with the air conditioner on. Her skin felt sticky under the silk fuchsia dress and matching linen jacket she'd put on in defiance of the surly day. Her calf-skin pumps, normally so comfortable, were too tight. She needed a cold drink and a blast of fresh air, and she needed them fast.

She pushed past the engraved bronze doors marked HOLCROFT & FARNSWORTH, stepped into the hushed lobby, and took a deep breath. The heat vanished along with the stink, the noise, and the too-sharp brightness. Relief flowed through her.

The security guard smiled and touched his hat. "Morning, Miss Merriman," he said.

Jocelyn smiled back. Behind the guard, in the polished surface of the elevator doors, she could see what he saw—a slender, elegant young woman in her late twenties with auburn hair in a graceful chignon, wide-spaced brown eyes, classic features, and particularly good legs.

She looked exactly like what she was supposed to be—well-bred, polished, perfectly at home in the rarified reaches of Holcroft & Farnsworth, auctioneers to the crème-de-la-so-much-crème it curdled if you looked at it wrong.

It was all fake, of course, but the guard had no way of knowing that. Neither did anyone else in the mahogany-paneled executive offices to which Jocelyn made her way. No one had ever heard of Josie Mulkowsky from Ozone Park, Queens. (Who in their right mind named a housing development after a poisonous gas?)

They certainly saw nothing of Josie in their esteemed colleague and fellow curator, "the lovely Jocelyn," as she'd been dubbed by Wilbur Holcroft himself, chairman of the firm and sometimes-benign paterfamilias.

Merriman was her mother's maiden name—Bertrice Merriman. Bertrice was the daughter of a nice young man from the Midwest who met a New York girl as he was passing through the Brooklyn navy yard on the way home from war.

One thing led to another, they married, a child was born, they divorced, mother and daughter remained in Brooklyn and in due course Bertrice met and married Sam Mulkowsky. They begot four children of their own, the eldest of whom was Jocelyn on her birth certificate but Josie to her family and friends.

In time, the family prospered, relatively speaking, in that it was no longer necessary to hoard nickels in the mason jar to buy shoes for the children. They moved to Ozone Park, the children grew and one of them—Jocelyn again—became a thing of wonder.

She went first to Columbia University on a scholarship, then to the Sorbonne with a year of additional study in Rome. She acquired a master's degree in the history of art, fluency in four languages, and a burning desire to make the love of her life her life's work. And there she ran up against a particularly unpleasant truth.

Very simply, Josie Mulkowsky didn't belong. She had no in, no kindly friend of the family to shepherd her across the threshold of the rarified sanctums she so longed to enter. After beating her head against that reality for a year and more, she stopped. She had reached the point in her life where she understood—really understood in the bone and sinew—that compromise was necessary.

She went back to school, a very exclusive school of her own devising in which she was both faculty and student. For six months, she studied the lives of the very rich in the same way she would study a particularly exciting work of art, painstakingly with a magnifying glass, so as to miss nothing.

When she was done, Josie Mulkowsky no longer existed except buried way down deep in the privacy of her own mind. In her place was Jocelyn Merriman, the lovely Jocelyn, beautiful, soignée, charming, and in her own elegant and gracious way quite a good art historian. Exactly the sort of person Wilbur Holcroft was only too happy to employ.

Lucky Jocelyn, happy Jocelyn, never mind that every time she walked through those bronze doors into that cool, hushed lobby, she felt a little twinge of fear that this would be the time the guard wouldn't smile but would instead tap her on the shoulder and point the way back to the steamy, fetid street, banishing her from whence she'd come.

But not today. She was safe again, upstairs in her corner office, with the air conditioner humming and a glass of iced tea with fresh spearmint leaves floating in it, just the thing to ease her dry throat.

"What's on for today?" she asked her secretary, Shelby Rutherford Whirling III, Trey to his friends. Very old family, the Whirlings, also the Rutherfords, maybe a tad too old and the blood running a bit thin, for while Trey was a nice enough guy and good-looking to boot, he was singularly lacking in ambition.

At twenty-three, with a degree from Harvard under his belt, he seemed perfectly happy making tea for Jocelyn and typing the occasional letter, both of which he did perfectly because that was simply how one did such things.

"Not much," he said. He stood, crisply perfect in a white Oxford shirt, Savile Row suit, polished brogues, and school tie, all six foot plus of blond, blue-eyed, upper-crust masculinity. For the life of her, Jocelyn couldn't figure out why she wasn't attracted to him. Granted he was six years her junior but that wouldn't exactly make her a cradle robber. And he did work for her but that was only temporary as his family background, if nothing else, assured he would be moving up.

No, there was something else, some lack of a necessary edge that kept her from indulging in any irregular thoughts about the pristine Trey. Let him make her tea and type her letters, it was enough.

"The Byzantine mosaics have arrived," he said. "They want to start the unpacking, but I said you'd have to be there."

Jocelyn nodded. "Good. We don't want any repeat of that van Gogh fiasco last year."

Trey grimaced. He hadn't actually been on staff the previous year when a van Gogh, in the process of being removed from its crate, was sufficiently mishandled to cause portions of the canvas to crack. The damage had been hastily repaired and the incident never made public. But it was the sort of possibility that haunted curators.

Impressionist painters weren't Jocelyn's field so she hadn't been directly involved. But she'd vowed to be even more careful with the beautiful, fragile antiquities she handled.

"Let's go," she said after a final sip of her tea. She stood with unmistakable enthusiasm. Opening the crates was always one of her favorite activities, no matter the need for caution. It was her idea of every birthday and Christmas morning rolled into one. Even when she knew exactly what would appear, she still gloried in that first precious glimpse of beauty so old it resonated with the dreams of a thousand generations of humanity.

Heady stuff but there was also the practical end of

checking condition and provenance, entering the items in the recently computerized firm inventory, and arranging for their storage within the cavernous vaults that took up a good part of the large, high-ceilinged basement.

The basement of Holcroft & Farnsworth—and the vaults within it—were legendary in the world of truly serious art collectors. It was said that even now there were objects piling up which the executives of the firm were convinced would enjoy enormous leaps in value in the coming years.

The firm could not only predict trends in art but manufacture them through a savvy mixture of rumor, innuendo, and outright promotion. A Matisse, purchased by Wilbur Holcroft for just over twenty thousand dollars in 1942, languished for more than forty years in the vaults.

Wilbur could have kept it on view in his office or one of his homes, but he understood that keeping it under wraps for so long would only add to its ultimate value. In 1989, it was removed at last and sold to the Japanese for six million cash.

Wondrous as the basement was, it had an almost medicinal quality to it. The lighting was starkly bright and the air antiseptically filtered. The effect was about as attractive as the average well-maintained morgue which it tended to resemble in its long banks of oversize stainless steel drawers, each neatly labeled with a description of whatever resided within.

Jocelyn did not linger. She confirmed that the mosaics —lifesize portraits of a sixth-century Byzantine merchant and his family that had adorned walls of their villa—were in excellent condition and lovely to boot with their sloe-eyed men and women gazing out in silent wonder. When they were safely secured in the vault to await the auction coming up the following month, she was glad enough to return upstairs.

It was getting on for lunchtime, but the thought of venturing out held no appeal. She settled for a chunky chicken salad sent in by the nearby deli. She was sitting at her desk, nibbling it, when the phone rang.

Trey was off duty, and the area outside the private offices was empty. Jocelyn reached for the phone. The small, commonplace action was absolutely without significance. She did it dozens of times each week and thought nothing of it.

But she should have—this time, in this place, in this instant just before the world of Jocelyn Merriman, aka Josie Mulkowsky, careened from its carefully constructed path and left her, like the inhabitants of the mosaics, caught within the fragments.

2

"**P**ax vobiscum," the old priest intoned. "Ite, missa est."

Actually, that wasn't what he said. Being a quite proper priest in this post-Vatican II world, he spread out his arms to the congregation and said in English, "Go in peace. The mass is ended."

It was Riordan Nolan's imagination working overtime that transformed the words back into their more mellifluous Latin, the Latin of his boyhood, when priests had really been somebody and you better not incur the wrath of God lest you end up a pillar of salt.

The good old days, back when he'd actually believed in something.

He stood up slowly and waited as a stooped, black-clad woman made her way out of the pew before he followed. As usual, there were more tourists in St. Patrick's Cathedral at that hour than there were celebrants for the mass. On Sundays, when the city's controversial cardinal mounted the pulpit, he packed them in. Otherwise, the big vaulted ceiling echoed to the click-click of Nikons and the drup-drup of sensible sneakers tromping up and down the marbled transept.

Off to one side in a small alcove of its own was a Pietà Riordan had always liked. It lacked the wrenching majesty of the Michelangelo but it was more comforting. He was staring at it, noting how the flickering flames of the memorial candles warmed the cold stone, when a hand touched his arm.

"Praying?" the man at his side asked with a slight smile.

"Thinking," Riordan replied. He took a step back and looked at the man. He was in his mid-thirties, tall and well-built with thick black hair, hazel eyes, and rugged features. There was a flush of healthy color in his cheeks. His manner was strong, self-assured, and pleasant.

He was a man people felt inclined to trust which was just as well, given his occupation. In his austere black cassock with the slash of white at the collar, he appeared in sharp contrast to the ornateness of the cathedral. And yet he was, as Riordan knew full well, at the very heart and soul of all it stood for.

The sight was disconcerting for it was almost himself he looked at, another self who had followed a wholly different path that had brought him to the cassock and the cathedral, to Holy Mother Church and to a lifetime of service in her name. The man was Riordan Nolan's fraternal twin brother, and they had not seen each other in over four years. Yet they did not embrace.

After a few moments of mutual study, Brendan Nolan motioned toward the small side door of the cathedral. "Let's step outside," he said.

Riordan went willingly enough. He found the atmosphere in the cathedral cloying. The combination of incense, ritual, and all those tourists depressed him. Outside was a raised garden that ran around the cathedral and adjacent rectory. It separated the religious from the secular and offered a measure of privacy, however fragile.

They sat on a bench beside a bed of ivy that looked as though it was wilting in the heat. Brendan's face flushed as soon as the warm, sticky air settled over him. Riordan remained unaffected. He was convinced that response to temperature was at least partly psychological.

In his case, he mentally compared every summer to the fetid, life-draining heat of the Mekong Delta with which he had been all too familiar twenty years before. By comparison, no whim of nature fazed him much today.

"It was actually cooler in Rome," Brendan said as he ran a finger around the inside of his collar.

"When did you leave?" Riordan asked.

"Two days ago. I had forgotten how New York can be."

It was ten years since Father Brendan Nolan had spent any appreciable time in the city of his birth. Tapped early for advancement within the church, he had spent most of the years since his ordination within the Vatican Palace. His responsibilities there had grown with his reputation until now it was whispered that he stood very close to the papal throne itself.

All this Riordan knew. He had followed his brother's career with interest but not surprise. Brendan had always been the cleverer of the two in certain ways, the one who knew what to say and when to say it.

He was unlike Riordan who tended to blunder his way through life, not particularly caring who he offended so long as the work got done and everything came out right in the end.

So far it had. At thirty-eight, he was at the top of his

profession, one of the most renowned antiquities experts in the country and well able to rival anything Europe or the Middle East could offer. He held a tenured position at Columbia University but his services were much in demand elsewhere.

He was one of those rare individuals who had a gift for the past. He could look at an object, hold it in his hands, even smell it, and immediately get a sense of where and how it had been made.

"What brings you here?" he asked his brother.

Brendan shrugged. He looked almost apologetic. "Business, what else?"

"The business of the church. Let's see, are you here to reprimand an errant priest, investigate a budding scandal, or vet a candidate for future office, making sure his theology is sufficiently unimaginative to pass muster?"

"Still the same old Riordan," Brendan said without rancor. Yet he felt called upon to add, "Mother Church has the right to protect herself. Indeed, it is a sacred duty."

"Mother Church has the right to serve God, whoever or whatever that may be," Riordan countered. "Self-preservation was never part of the contract. Self-aggrandizement most certainly isn't."

Was it a trick of the light or did his brother seem to flinch? "Ah, yes," Brendan murmured, "the contract or more correctly, the covenant. God bestowed it on Abraham at the stone of sacrifice, confirmed it with Moses at Sinai, and made it living flesh in the Messiah. What makes you so certain you know its terms when the rest of us don't share that confidence?"

Riordan's eyebrows rose. There were some who said they were his most expressive feature, being thick, black, and assertive. "Doubt, brother? I didn't know your mind stretched to it these days."

"There is always doubt. Only a fool lives without it. What counts is faith and mine is immutable." The priest in him added, "I only wish the same could be said for you."

Riordan looked away, staring into the too-bright bowl of the sky. "I prefer uncertainty. It's more interesting."

"If you say so." Brendan paused, as though considering his course of action. He had the air of a man who has surveilled the same ground several times but feels compelled to take one final look before crossing it.

"I need your help," he said finally.

Riordan's eyes narrowed. He could not remember the last time his brother had asked for his assistance in anything.

When they were children, the twenty minutes that separated their births had been enough for Riordan to covet the role of big brother, but insufficient for Brendan to grant it to him. Closely resembling each other yet far from identical they had gone their separate ways without any great regret. With each passing year, there seemed less to bind them.

And yet suddenly here was Father Brendan Nolan of Holy Mother Church reaching out to his renegade brother for help.

"What the hell's wrong?" Riordan demanded. For Brendan to turn to him, it had to be something major. The sudden thought of his brother in trouble twisted inside him.

"Interesting choice of words," Brendan said. His smile was wry.

"The hell of it, brother, is that the church finds itself in a situation of potential embarrassment which also, conveniently enough, happens to be right up your alley. It seems that several weeks ago, there was a theft from the Vatican archives. The object taken has no special significance, but just the fact that it could be removed raises all sorts of questions about our security. As you undoubtedly know, many wealthy and influential people, true friends of the Church, have generously given objects of great value to the Vatican collection. Were they to believe that such gifts were being treated cavalierly, it would not sit well. You follow?"

"Sort of. Something was stolen and you don't want people to know about it. What's that got to do with me?"

"The stolen object was a manuscript dating to the early Christian era. It's a rehashing of other, far more important documents by the Church fathers so we don't particularly care about its disappearance. But if word gets out that the Vatican is ripe for the plundering, we could end up in a nasty position. Since you're an acknowledged expert in that area, I proposed enlisting your help to locate the document and, hopefully, the thieves. With the proper discouragement, we can put an end to any future problems before they begin."

"I see," Riordan said slowly. In fact, he didn't or at least not completely. An early Christian era document? Okay, he could understand that and understand why he'd be called in to look for it. With his contacts throughout the antiquities world, he'd be a logical choice even if his brother weren't a high-ranking priest.

But a document from that period that was of no particular importance? That was harder to believe. Anything that old was automatically valuable, at least to people who cared about such things.

"What is the document?" he asked.

"As I said, a rehashing of basic information we already have in far more fluent form. What counts is the breach of security."

"You say the theft occurred several weeks ago?"

Brendan nodded. "I regret not coming to you immediately but we thought we could handle it through our own channels. Unfortunately, we've hit a dead end. If the thieves had been Italian, or European of any sort, or even American, we would have located them by now. Unfortunately, we've come to believe that they're Middle Eastern. Our contacts in that part of the world remain tenuous."

"I should think so," Riordan murmured. Did his brother realize what he was saying? Thieves of Middle Eastern origin invading the Vatican archives to steal a document of no particular importance? Oh, sure, that happened all the time.

"They just waltzed into the archives and helped themselves to a document nobody cared about? Why didn't they take something of actual value?"

"They were interrupted. The scroll in question was kept in a gold and ivory cylinder which may be what drew their attention. The end caps are decorated with turtledoves, by the way, in case you happen to come across it."

He paused for a moment before he said, "Look, the point is we want to get through to these people that they can't do this sort of thing. We think they'll attempt to sell the scroll. It's possible that anyone interested in buying it might come to you for authentication."

"It's possible," Riordan agreed, "but not likely. There are plenty of people around who could authenticate an early Christian document."

"Perhaps, but you're the best. We're betting it's you they'll contact."

"Why?" Riordan demanded. He didn't like the way this was going. There was something his brother wasn't saying. "Why would I be sought out to authenticate a perfectly ordinary document?"

Brendan hesitated. Clearly, he did not want to say it but equally clearly he was going to have to. "We think the thieves may make outlandish claims about the scroll in order to hype its price. They'd be lying, of course, but that doesn't matter. Under those circumstances, any possible buyer would be inclined to seek out the top expert in the field."

"The top man is Daniel Levinson. He's retired from Tel Aviv University."

"Sadly, Professor Levinson suffered a stroke last month and is not expected to recover."

That was news to Riordan, and he was sorry to hear it. Levinson was in his nineties and had long since retired to private life, but he was still held in great respect.

"What about Diana Schultz?"

"Excavating somewhere in the wilds of northern Turkey and unreachable."

"You have done your homework," Riordan said thoughtfully. This was more than a matter of brother helping brother. Brendan had made sure he was coming to the right place.

"It's an important matter. The church has an absolute responsibility to protect what has been entrusted to it. Whatever your feelings about the theology, you must understand that."

Riordan nodded slowly. "I understand it."

"Then you'll help?"

"I'll do what I can, but I still think the odds are slim that I'll be contacted."

"Perhaps you're right," Brendan said. He stood up and reached into one of the hidden pockets of his cassock. The white card he handed Riordan was of the finest quality and embossed with the papal seal. "I'll be returning to Rome this evening. You can reach me there at these numbers any time."

"Night or day?" Riordan asked, half facetiously.

"Yes," his brother said, quite seriously, "night or day."

They parted a few minutes later, Brendan through the side door of the cathedral and Riordan back onto the street. Fifth Avenue was emptier than usual. He strolled along, hands in his pockets, and thought about the meeting.

His brother looked good and sounded confident but there was an undercurrent of anxiety that was out of character. Brendan had never been one to agonize over anything. Part of his success in life was due to the assumption he projected that nothing would go wrong for him. Now it seemed something had, and maybe not just for one priest.

Riordan turned, squinting against the sun, and stared at the spires of the cathedral. A single chime rang out from the great bells, signaling the first hour after noon. Following on it came the soft, mournful strains of "Agnus Dei, lamb of God."

Riordan turned away. He did not want to think of lambs, of sacrifice, or of whatever his brother was trying to involve him in. The conviction was growing in him that he would know soon enough.

3

"Miss Merriman," the man on the other end of the phone said, "my name is Hassan Saleem. Am I correct in thinking that you are the antiquities curator for Holcroft & Farnsworth?"

The accent was Middle Eastern, Syrian perhaps or Lebanese. The English was fluent. Jocelyn pulled a notepad toward her and jotted down the name.

"Yes, you are, Mr. Saleem. How may I help you?"

"I have an artifact I believe may interest you. I wish to offer it for private sale."

Private sale meant not at auction. Mr. Saleem was seeking to use the offices of Holcroft & Farnsworth as a broker or agent. It was not an unusual arrangement.

The firm held a major antiquities auction only once a year, the most recent having been barely two months before. Lacking an entire collection to offer, rather than a single piece, he would have to wait almost a year. By going private, he avoided the delay and eluded the glare of publicity that sometimes attended such auctions.

"I see," Jocelyn said. "Very well. Where are you located at the moment?"

She had a sense the call was local but it was difficult to tell these days. Sometimes it was easier to talk to someone in Athens than it was to get a clear connection ten blocks away.

"New York," Mr. Saleem said. "But only temporarily. I will be leaving shortly. I would like to have your appraisal as quickly as possible."

"All right," Jocelyn said. "I can see it this afternoon, if you like. I'm usually here during business hours and sometimes afterward. What would be convenient for you?"

"I am sorry," Mr. Saleem said, and he sounded as though he meant it. "I am not prepared to transport the artifact. You must come to it."

Jocelyn hesitated. Granted, it was hardly unheard of for a curator to work on-site, as it were. Wealthy and privileged clients expected that sort of treatment as a matter of course. But Mr. Saleem was an unknown as was his artifact.

"That may be difficult," Jocelyn hedged. "Where are you exactly?"

He hesitated a moment before giving an address near Mulberry Street in lower Manhattan. It was a neighborhood of meat butchers, pawn shops, wary residents, and four-story walk-ups that almost qualified as antiquities themselves. After dark, it was well-known for another kind of meat market consisting of five-dollars-a-pop hookers of both sexes and every possible variation in between.

"I'm sorry," Jocelyn said firmly, "but that is impossible. You will have to bring the object here."

"I cannot," Mr. Saleem said with equal firmness.

Again, he hesitated. His voice dropped a notch. "Miss Merriman, we are speaking of an extremely rare and important artifact. It would be a tragedy to have it fall into the wrong hands. I must be extremely careful."

If he wanted to be careful, Jocelyn thought, he should be living somewhere other than a gang-ridden neighborhood—and Chinese gangs at that, from the neighboring Chinatown. On the other hand, it wasn't impossible that he had chosen it deliberately. He sounded cultured, educated, and—if it was possible to tell such a thing—prosperous. It might be a case of his wanting to be in the last place anyone who knew him would think to look.

Or he might be a con man, a crook, or worse. Her antennae were up but they were wiggling indecisively.

"What exactly are we talking about, Mr. Saleem?"

Whoever he was, he knew the use of the pregnant pause. After an appropriate interval, he said, "You have heard of the Magdalen Scroll?"

Jocelyn tossed down her pencil and pushed the pad away. She eyed the salad she had abandoned for this nuisance call.

"The Magdalen Scroll," she said briskly, "is nothing more than a legend, like the Holy Grail or the Sword of Arthur. It doesn't exist. You are wasting my time, Mr. Saleem."

Far from being offended by such bluntness, he chuckled softly. "On the contrary, Miss Merriman. I am offering you possibly the greatest coup in antiquities in this century or, for that matter, any other. The Magdalen Scroll is real, it exists, and it is in my possession. It is my intention to sell it, if not through Holcroft & Farnsworth, then through some other agent. Should you wish to prevent that, I will expect you at 6:00 P.M."

Before Jocelyn could reply, the phone went dead. She put the receiver down slowly. It was crazy, absurd, a total waste of time. There was no such thing as the Magdalen Scroll. And yet—

She took a deep breath and for just a moment let her imagination go. If Saleem was telling her the truth and the scroll really did exist—and if it was what legend claimed—then it would indeed be an antiquity find of enormous importance. But no, it was impossible. She might as well go searching for the fountain of youth or the lost mines of King Solomon.

Or she might walk down the hall and have a word about it with Wilbur Holcroft.

He was there, as usual, ensconced in the big wing chair beside the floor-to-ceiling windows that looked out over the avenue. The room was purely Wilbur, a no-holds-barred indulgence in the seventeenth- and eighteenth-century style he favored, claiming it represented the highest attainment of human civilization from which everything had gone steadily downhill.

There were those who doubted Wilbur ever left the office, virtually living in the suite that included a bedroom, bath, and private dining room. He had a magnificent home in Greenwich, Connecticut, another in the British Virgin Islands, and a third in the south of France. But in his seventy-seventh year with virtually every thrill life had to offer experienced numerous times over, he seemed to prefer being at the hub of the firm that was his proudest accomplishment.

"Do you have a moment?" Jocelyn asked.

He swung round in the chair. "For you? Of course."

In his youth, Wilbur had been regarded as regrettably plain. In middle age, he became almost aggressively ugly.

But in what he referred to as the "goddamn twilight of my years" he had taken on an odd sort of beauty. His skin was as smooth and unlined as a baby's, his eyes glowed, and his hairless dome shone pink and freckled.

"Come in," Wilbur said. He gestured to the couch beside him. "It's been a week and more since I saw you. What have you been up to?"

"Arranging for the Byzantine mosaics. They arrived today and they really are lovely."

"I'll have to take a look," Wilbur said but she doubted that he would. These days, he rarely ventured into the great vaults below ground. It seemed enough for him simply to know that they were kept pleasantly full.

"That isn't what brings you here," he said. "Something's troubling you."

She smiled ruefully. "Is it that obvious?"

"Definitely. You're like most people who have a genuine gift for the rare and beautiful. You are almost always securely focused in that direction with the result that very little distracts you. But now something has changed." He looked hopeful. "It wouldn't be a man, would it?"

Wilbur had been trying for several years to convince Jocelyn that a woman of her qualities should have a life beyond work. So far he hadn't succeeded.

"Afraid not," she said. "I received a phone call a short time ago from a man who identified himself as Hassan Saleem. Have you ever heard of him?"

Wilbur shook his head. "Doesn't ring a bell. What did he want?"

"He claims he has the Magdalen Scroll."

The look of dumbfounded amazement that crossed Wilbur's face almost made the whole exercise worthwhile. "You jest."

Jocelyn shrugged. She had to admit that saying it out loud made it seem even more ridiculous. "That's what he says."

"He actually told you he is in possession of the scroll?"

Jocelyn nodded. "He wants me to come down and see it this evening."

"Come where?"

When she told him, he shook his head. "That's a rather unappetizing neighborhood, don't you think?"

"It occurred to me he might be hiding out there."

"I suppose, or he could be one of your garden-variety crazies who do so well around here."

"True," Jocelyn said. "So you think I shouldn't go?"

Wilbur pressed his fingers together and stared at her over them. "I didn't say that exactly. The Magdalen Scroll . . ." His eyes took on a faraway look. "It's only legend, of course, but—"

"But if there was any chance that it actually existed, it would be worth moving heaven and earth to acquire it."

"One might very well have to move them. The Magdalen Scroll, if real, would not merely be worth a great deal of money, it would be potentially explosive. I find it difficult to believe that the gentlemen at the Vatican wouldn't be determined to acquire it for themselves."

"I can understand their interest," Jocelyn said, "but considering the extent of early Christian era documents they already possess, they might consider one more unnecessary."

Wilbur looked at her skeptically. "Dear child, think what you're saying. The Magdalen Scroll is supposed to be the eyewitness testament of Mary Magdalen regarding what she saw as a follower of Jesus Christ. Not only might it throw aspects of Christian theology into doubt, it also raises the issue of women's position in the church. To say the least, it would be an extremely hot potato."

"Then perhaps the firm shouldn't be involved."

"Nonsense. Since when has Holcroft & Farnsworth been afraid of controversy? Granted, there's probably nothing to it but if you insist on finding out, I wouldn't stand in your way."

Jocelyn hadn't insisted on any such thing but the message was clear all the same. If there was any chance—no matter how slim—that the Magdalen Scroll was real, she should do everything possible to secure it.

And everything most definitely included a trip to Mulberry Street.

She arrived five minutes before the allotted time and asked the cabdriver if he would wait. He looked at her with mild interest, as though the sight of a truly crazy person enlivened his day some small degree.

"Whatta ya, nuts?"

"I'll double the meter."

"Ya gotta be kiddin'. There's nothing down here but winos and dealers. I sit here more than two minutes, my cab'll end up stripped."

"Triple," Jocelyn said. She edged from one foot to the other and tried not to sound impatient.

"I got three kids an' an ol' lady with varicose veins ya wouldn't believe. She stands for more than a couple of minutes, she's finished for the day. So I lose my cab, maybe I get mugged in the process, and for what?"

"A hundred bucks," Jocelyn said. "That's what a limo down here would cost. Take it or leave it."

"A hun'red and fifty."

"Highway robbery."

"I'm outta here."

"Wait! Okay, a hundred and fifty." Jeez, it might as well still be the 1980s when money was water. "But I want a receipt." She'd send the bill for this one to Wilbur personally.

"Yeah, yeah. How long ya gonna be?"

"Not long. I'll be in that building right over there." She pointed to make sure he got it. If she didn't return in a reasonable length of time, she wanted somebody to know where to send the cops.

"Suit yerself, lady." He rolled up the windows, snapped all the doors locked, and kept the motor running.

Jocelyn couldn't blame him. She had a bad feeling about the whole thing. The neighborhood was as raunchy as she'd expected. The building Saleem had directed her to looked as though it was falling down, and the little hairs on the back of her neck were telling her she had no business being here.

Except that she did. Firm business, the kind of thing that kept her in her corner office with the spearmint leaves in her tea and her dream-come-true job.

But then there were days when Ozone Park didn't seem too bad.

She checked the address again on the off chance it was actually for someplace uptown. It wasn't. Gingerly, she crossed the street, opened the door, and found the right apartment bell. Her finger shook slightly as she pushed it.

4

Hassan Saleem was a man in his mid-fifties, of medium height, with swarthy skin, dark hair, and a beautifully cultivated moustache. He was waiting for Jocelyn as she got off the freight elevator, the only means of conveyance in the former warehouse. Other such buildings in other neighborhoods had been turned into luxurious condominiums filled with prestige lofts. This one had not.

Yet Saleem was making do. He occupied the topmost floor, all of it, with high windows looking out over the street and a rickety steel staircase leading to the roof for an easy means of escape. A few walls had been thrown up, a simple kitchen installed, the floor carpeted, and some relatively good furniture moved in. It wasn't plush but it was a surprise considering its surroundings.

"Not bad," Jocelyn said. "Do you stay here often?"

He hesitated. The tendency to carefully consider anything he said apparently went beyond the telephone. "When the need arises. May I offer you a drink? I have a very nice white Burgundy I can recommend."

"Thank you but no. Mineral water would be fine."

Saleem had three kinds, also little slices of lime to put in it. He fixed the same for himself. They sat down opposite each other on the overstuffed Haitian cotton couches.

"Thank you for coming," he said gravely.

"I hope you understand that I will need proof of your claims regarding the Magdalen Scroll." No point beating around the bush.

"Of course. I would expect nothing less."

He stood up, went over to a nearby wall unit, and removed a leather folder of the type executives carried to meetings to conceal their regulation yellow legal-size notepads.

From the folder, he withdrew a single sheet of paper and handed it to Jocelyn.

"What is this?" she asked.

"A photocopy of a portion of the scroll. I offer it to you so that you may authenticate the language, script, and so on. I also believe you will find the contents of interest. Once that is done, we may proceed to the next step."

Jocelyn fingered the photocopy dubiously. "It was my understanding when I came down here that I would see the scroll itself. Otherwise, to be quite frank, I would not have come."

"You will see it," Hassan assured her, "but you must understand that security is my primary concern. There are unscrupulous people who would go to great lengths to secure the scroll."

"Perhaps," Jocelyn said. "But I have a great many questions to ask about how *you* came into possession of such a legendary artifact."

Hassan smiled. He gestured to the photocopy. "All in good time, Miss Merriman. But first, I need to be assured of your interest and you need to be convinced there is something to be interested in."

"A photocopy proves nothing. Script, language, syntax, all the necessary elements can be faked by someone skillful enough. You would do better to show me the actual scroll."

"That is out of the question. I am not yet prepared to reveal its whereabouts and even if I were, it is far too valuable a document to risk transporting myself. When the time comes for it to be moved, I trust Holcroft & Farnsworth to have the appropriate resources."

In point of fact, Holcroft & Farnsworth had the resources to move just about anything anywhere in the world and to do it with the utmost confidentiality and safety. Such service was merely a sideline of the firm but a valuable one.

"All right," Jocelyn said slowly. "I will see what I can do with this. When can I get back to you?"

"Within forty-eight hours," Saleem said, "no longer."

"That's impossible. It could take me a week or more to find someone to do the authentication and then that person will need time."

Saleem shook his head. He looked sincerely regretful but he did not relent. "Forty-eight hours, no more. I have obligations that prevent me from remaining longer."

"Then I will contact you wherever you are going to be."

Saleem sighed. He set his glass aside and looked at her solemnly. "Miss Merriman, you are, by all repute, a woman of intelligence and sophistication. Obviously, if I were willing to give you a forwarding address, I would do so. But I am not. Put plainly, I value my privacy."

He pronounced the last word in the British style as though speaking of a privet hedge. It did not seem an

affectation. Mr. Saleem appeared to be one of those people who was at home almost everywhere but with ties to
nowhere.

"All right," Jocelyn said reluctantly. "Forty-eight hours.
But if I can't get back to you by then, I hope you will be
in touch with me again."

Saleem shrugged as though to say all such things were
in the hands of a higher power. Jocelyn stayed a short
time before making the return trip down in the freight
elevator. She felt tired and irritated. The whole trip
seemed like a waste of time. Photostat, indeed!

To her relief, the cab was still there. She jumped into it,
slammed the door shut and told the driver to take her
back to Holcroft & Farnsworth. The sooner she got
started, the better.

By 10:00 P.M., she had a list made of all her possible
alternatives. Daniel Levinson's name was at the top; she
did not yet know about his stroke. There were half a
dozen others, some with question marks beside them because although they were good, they might not be good
enough for something that claimed to be the Magdalen
Scroll.

At the bottom of the list, with no question mark beside
it, was Riordan Nolan's name. She had added him reluctantly, having her own reasons for not wanting to deal
with him.

That done, she turned to the photocopy itself. It was a
standard size page, eight and a half by eleven inches, but
the top and bottom margins were blank. Within it, mea-
suring about eight inches in depth, was the actual copy. It
was possible to see the thin horizontal lines where it began and ended, as well as a slight darkening of the paper
corresponding to the darker color of the scroll. There

were two columns of twenty lines each written in a cunei-
form script.

Jocelyn squinted as she looked at it. Her languages included Ancient Greek and Latin, as required for an antiquities scholar, but this was neither. She got up, rummaged
around in the books that lined one wall of her office, and
found what she was looking for. The volume was heavy,
bound in leather, and had that look of weighty substance
all scholarly works aim for. The spine said: *Aramaic
Grammar and Vocabulary*.

Aramaic was the language spoken in the Holy Land
during the early Christian period. It was a very old and
long-enduring tongue, still spoken by a small number of
people in the Middle East. Jocelyn had heard a scholar at
Harvard give a brief talk in it and although she could not
understand the words, she had been struck by the particular beauty of their sound.

She set the book beside the photocopy and began com-
paring them. Even to her untutored eye, it appeared that
the language in the copy could be Aramaic. However, she
couldn't begin to translate it. The script was too complex
and in places too faded for her to even make the attempt.
Still, she was satisfied that the first, most basic hurdle had
been overcome: the scroll was not an immediate and obvious forgery.

That brought her back to the problem of authenticating
it. It was too late to call anyone local and too early to call
elsewhere. She'd have to sleep on it. Which was just as
well. She was bone tired. The day begun with tea and
mosaics had taken a strange, ominous turn.

All her previous dealings on behalf of the firm had been
fairly straightforward. This was not. There still remained

the strong possibility that the whole thing was a scam. Or, almost worse, the scroll could be real but stolen.

Sorting out its provenance, where it came from and who had legal right to it, would be as important as determining whether or not it was authentic. She told herself she was up to that challenge but she had her doubts.

She went down the hall to Wilbur's office. It was vacant and no light shone from beneath the door leading to his bedroom. Either he wasn't there or he was already asleep.

Quietly, she went to the wall safe behind his desk. It was concealed by a particularly lovely if modest Matisse. A year before, in recognition of her service to the firm and the high position of trust she had attained, Wilbur had given her the combination. She used it now to open the safe. With the photocopy stashed away, she locked up securely and left. An hour later, she was home in her apartment, in bed with the air conditioner whirring.

Sleep came more easily than she expected but her dreams were troubling. They were full of sloe-eyed people, black-clad, walking beneath tolling bells, and far in the background the sound of laughter tumbling off cathedral spires.

About the best that could be said was that she awoke to the sound of rain. The heat wave had broken and the city was getting a much-needed shower. She dressed, ate a quick piece of toast washed down by the lethal black coffee she indulged in once a day, and fumbled in the back of her closet for her raincoat. Outside the streets were awash with hurrying pedestrians, crawling traffic, the usual cacophony of horns and brakes hooting and squealing.

She got into the office to find that Trey was out with a head cold. First on her mental list of do's was to update Wilbur, but he wasn't to be found. That moved her right on to number two, digging up an expert on early Christian era documents.

Digging up turned out to be a poor choice of words. She winced as she drew a line through Daniel Levinson's name. What a shame. He was the grand old man of the field and someone she would have been delighted to call upon for help. But a phone call to his residence outside of Haifa brought the information that he was "comfortable but fading."

Jocelyn had attended a seminar of his one summer in Greece. She remembered him saying that if there was anything to the idea of reincarnation, he wanted to come back as a noble in the court of King Solomon, a time he regarded as being particularly civilized and enjoyable. Jocelyn hoped he would get his wish.

She moved on down the list, scratching out names as she went. It was amazing how many of these people were occupied at the far reaches of the earth, or simply out of touch, or in one case, institutionalized. Ah, well, no one ever said the urge to delve into the distant past was a sign of robust mental health.

That left Riordan Nolan. His mental health was excellent despite what were rumored to have been hellish experiences in Vietnam. He had no patience for ineptitude or laziness, but everyone agreed he was a superb scholar and teacher.

There was a problem in that he had written a scathing article several years before for *The New York Times Magazine* in which he struck out at the art and auction world, charging that antiquities were routinely looted, sold illegally, and hidden away in private collections where they were useless to serious researchers.

The article hadn't won him any friends at Holcroft &

Farnsworth, or indeed at any other auction house. Wilbur would not be at all pleased to have him involved.

But Wilbur would survive. The question was, would Jocelyn? She remembered Riordan Nolan all too clearly from her own days at Columbia when she'd been a starry-eyed undergraduate and he the golden boy of the antiquities faculty.

She'd audited one of his graduate seminars. They'd gone out for coffee. They'd gone home together. It was the one and only time in her life she had done such a thing. The next day, Riordan got word that the grant he'd been looking for to dig in Anatolia had come through and a week later he was gone.

She told herself it didn't matter, they'd been two ships passing in the night, a brief encounter, all that crap. It didn't work. For longer than she cared to admit, she'd gone around alternately missing Riordan Nolan and wishing she'd never laid eyes on him.

Now he was safely stowed away in her memory, deep enough where he couldn't bother her anymore, which was just the way she wanted it. But he was also the only name left on her list.

For the second time in two days, she faced a decision she didn't want to make. Time was ticking by, she had to do something, and it looked like Riordan might be the only game in town. She called the university to make sure he was there but made no attempt to speak to him directly.

With the photocopy back in her purse, she snagged a cab and headed uptown. It was still pouring, which suited her mood. She wished she'd never heard of the Magdalen Scroll, Hassan Saleem, or any of it. She wished she was somebody else in an entirely different place. She wished—

To hell with it. The cab veered in toward the curb, throwing up a shower of water, and jerked to a stop. She paid the driver and jumped back just in time to avoid being soaked as he drove off.

Ten minutes later, having found her way to Riordan's office, she ignored the frantic little brain cells that were screaming at her to turn back, raised her hand, and knocked firmly on the door.

5

The woman looked familiar. She stood in the doorway of his office, wearing a flowing cerulean blue raincoat tightly belted at the waist, with a silk scarf covering her hair, all slender elegance and cool beauty while Riordan tried to figure out where he knew her from.

He drew a blank but he was sure it was temporary. He *knew* her, or at least his subconscious did. The rest of him would follow along eventually.

"May I help you?" he asked, nicely because he was at heart a courteous man, equally gracious to little old ladies, cleaning women, and the tiny Indian seamstress at the dry cleaner who always sewed the buttons back on his shirts.

The woman smiled. She took a few steps into the office and held out her hand. "I hope so. My name is Jocelyn Merriman. I represent the firm of Holcroft & Farnsworth. We would like to obtain your services to authenticate an early Christian era document."

That's what she said; what she was thinking was altogether different. It went like this: The creep, the big, dumbheaded, no-good creep. How dare he not recognize me?

And right along with that, running side by side, was this: Thank God, I don't have to tell him if I don't want to. It's kind of funny actually, my knowing something he doesn't. How far can I play this?

Meanwhile, Riordan was doing his own thinking. The moment she opened her mouth, he was more convinced than ever that he knew her but he still couldn't put it together. Besides, a woman like this he wouldn't have forgotten, would he?

All that notwithstanding, a burst of energy zapped through him when she said what she wanted. It could be a coincidence except he didn't believe in them, and his gut was telling him now wasn't the time to start. Old Brendan had been right on target after all.

"Sit down, Miss Merriman," he said. He hefted a stack of books off the chair across from his desk and added them to all the other stacks sprinkled around the floor.

"You're welcome to tell me what this is about," he went on, "but I don't do much in the way of authentications, especially not for outfits like Holcroft & Farnsworth."

"I know your position on the sale of antiquities," Jocelyn said calmly. "You've been very vocal about it." Indeed, she could remember him talking about the subject the only time they'd had dinner together.

"But you have to admit that not all works of art can end up in museums. Some are going to be sold to private collectors. Holcroft & Farnsworth has always been scrupulous in its attention to provenance. We do not involve ourselves in a transaction unless we are certain that the seller has legal ownership."

He sat back in his chair, stretched out his long legs, and

put his eyebrows together. "Yeah, right. What about that Etruscan urn last year?"

Jocelyn flushed. She could feel it happening, hated it, but couldn't stop it. Trust him to know about the urn. And to have the gall to mention it.

It had happened while she was on vacation. An assistant curator who was frankly gunning for Jocelyn's job took consignment of an Etruscan urn that she swore was provenanced up the kazoo. She didn't put it that way, being from Bryn Mawr, but what she did say amounted to the same thing.

The only problem was that it wasn't. This particular Etruscan urn had been stolen from a prominent German Jewish family during World War II. It turned up in the possession of a supposed Swiss who sold it to an up-and-coming Italian businessman. The businessman kept it in his villa near Naples until it was stolen again, this time by thieves working on commission for an American industrialist who had a thing for Etruscan, plus didn't like the Italian.

The American kept it for five years before he died in a plane crash that was still under investigation. At that point, the urn went to the museum the industrialist had founded in his name except that it didn't. During the transfer, it disappeared yet again, stolen for the third time in fifty years.

Forget provenance, the urn might as well have been a magnet for thieves, nut-case collectors, and all the other unsavory folks Wilbur really did prefer not to deal with.

Jocelyn ferreted out the truth, got the assistant axed, and saw to it that the urn eventually made its way back to the sole surviving cousin of the original owners. Score one for her but it didn't change anything. Riordan had made his point.

"Very unfortunate," she said, "but even the best-regulated organization will have occasional problems. That's why I'm here now. A first-century Aramaic scroll may be coming onto the market. If we are to handle it, we must make absolutely sure what we're dealing with."

Riordan shrugged. He was trying hard to look like he didn't care much when in fact he was getting excited. He was sure Brendan hadn't leveled with him. Whatever the scroll was, there was more to it than his brother had said.

Some men got a charge out of reeling in a four-hundred-pound marlin. Others got it shooting deer or geese or quail, or any of the other helpless things people liked to hunt down and kill.

Riordan got his putting together little pieces of the past, fragments of an enormous jigsaw puzzle that would never be completed but which gave tantalizing clues as to how—and maybe even why—the human race had gotten into its present situation.

"Okay," he said, still working on casual, "I'll take a look. Got it with you?"

"No," Jocelyn said, with that little edge in her voice that said she was prepared to be patient but let's not overdo it. "I have a photocopy of a section of the scroll."

"Then you've got nothing."

"It's a start," she insisted. "The contact says the scroll itself can be viewed after we confirm our interest. Before I can do that, I want to know what you make of the copy." For good measure, she added, "It is written in Aramaic. I've confirmed that for myself."

Riordan looked at her skeptically. "You know Aramaic?"

"No, but I got out a book and compared samples with what's written on the section we have. They look similar."

He rolled his eyes. "If that's a sample of how you people check on things, it's no wonder the antiquities business is in so much trouble." He held out his hand. "Give it here."

She gave him her best cold-eyed stare, snapped open her purse, and removed the photocopy. Riordan glanced at it, prepared to say right off the bat that it wasn't Aramaic, was Hindi maybe, and nothing to do with anything.

Except that he couldn't. It was Aramaic and of the kind common in the first century A.D. Moreover, the particular form of writing looked correct too. On top of all that, a word or two caught his eye and made him sit upright in the chair.

There was a reference to a village he knew to be near the old town of Nazareth and another to the house of a man named—He looked closer, trying to make it out, but the exact transcription eluded him. This was going to take work.

"When do you need this by?"

"Tomorrow."

He looked up sharply, meeting her brown eyes. There was something about those eyes—

"You're kidding?"

"Afraid not. The client, or at least the possible client, is most insistent."

"That's crazy."

"So I told him but he's a busy man."

"Has it occurred to you there might be some other reason for his wanting you to bite so quick?"

"Yes," Jocelyn said. "The goods may be a forgery or

they may be stolen. I have to eliminate both possibilities before Holcroft could begin to look for a buyer."

Riordan wasn't sure why, but he believed her. He still had all the same deeply held reservations about secreting antiquities away in private collections, but he was willing to give Miss Jocelyn Merriman the benefit of the doubt. She seemed on the level when she said she didn't want to do anything illegal.

That meant she didn't know about the theft, and he wasn't about to tell her. At least not until he had a whole lot better idea what he was dealing with.

He glanced again at the two columns of script. They were not particularly well written, as though the hand holding the stylus hadn't been overly familiar with its task. There were several scratchings out with words squeezed in between lines. Not the work of a professional scribe then. That made it all the more interesting.

He looked up again, surprised to see that Jocelyn was still there. Already his mind was firmly on the fragment and the puzzle it represented.

"I'll get back to you in the morning."

Jocelyn slipped a business card from her purse and laid it on the desk. "I'll be waiting to hear from you."

She let herself out, fully aware that he did not notice her go. Whatever chagrin she felt was overwhelmed by the unexpected sense of relief. For better or worse, it seemed she had come to the right place.

Several events took place in the hours immediately after Jocelyn left Riordan's office:

Hassan Saleem received a call from an associate in Damascus that upset him sufficiently to require a larger than usual dose of the Valium that had become his constant companion of late. Because he believed in preparing for all possible contingencies, he sat down at his desk and wrote a brief letter.

There was a postbox directly in front of his building, otherwise he would not have ventured out at night to mail the letter. That done, he returned to the apartment where he watched the *Tonight* show, trying once again to discern what its appeal might be, and eventually drifted into sleep.

About the same time, Wilbur Holcroft returned to his office and went immediately to his safe. It was not precisely empty—there were a pair of ten-carat canary diamonds he intended to have set as earrings for his favorite grandniece's upcoming wedding, a sixteenth-century map by the great cartographer, Gerardus Mercator, and a rare letter personally written by President Andrew Jackson who had not been known for the frequency of his correspondence except through his far more literate secretaries.

However, there was no photocopy of a fragment of a first-century Aramaic scroll.

Wilbur sat down at his inlaid chestnut and mahogany desk and tapped his fingers. He did not like this at all. It would force him to do something and if there was one thing he disliked at his age, it was having to act. He felt he had earned the privilege of inertia and resented being roused from it. He was frowning as he set about contemplating what to do.

By contrast, Father Brendan Riordan looked perfectly serene, but then he almost always did. Dressed in his customary black cassock, he stood at the small altar off the center basilica of St. Peter's. His hands were clasped before him, his eyes lowered.

The great bells of the cathedral were silent and the choir was absent, but in his heart he heard the soaring notes of the "Kyrie Eleison. Lord, have mercy." Those words, uttered so routinely in every Catholic church around the world, held a special significance for Brendan Nolan. They were, in some immutable way, his personal challenge hurled in the face of doubt and despair. While there was breath in his body, he would never allow anything to diminish them.

"This is my blood," he recited, raising the cup and holding it before the cross. "Drink of it in remembrance of me."

He closed his eyes and pressed the cup to his lips.

6

Riordan didn't wait until the following morning to call Jocelyn. He called her home number shortly after midnight. There were two reasons for this. The first was that he had completed the translation of the fragment. The second was that he had remembered who she was.

"Hi, Josie," he said when she picked up the phone.

"That didn't take long," she replied. Ordinarily, she would have been asleep at that hour but the events of the day had her mind working overtime. Rather than toss and turn in bed, she was sitting on a stool at the kitchen counter eating chocolate ice cream straight from the container and reading about Mary Magdalen.

The Bible didn't have much to say about her really. She got surprisingly little mention considering that she was one of the best known figures in Christianity. Fortunately, there were other sources that went into far more detail about her.

"You had me going for a while," Riordan said.

Jocelyn put down the translation of the Gnostic Gospels

she'd been studying and said, "Confess, Nolan, you didn't have a clue."

"It was the nose job that threw me."

"Nose job! What're you talking about? I didn't have any nose job."

"Then what happened to the cute little bump?"

"It's still right there where it always was. You didn't look closely enough. Or maybe your memory's not as good as you think it is."

For good measure, and just to make sure he knew where they stood, she said, "After all, it's not as though we knew each other especially well."

There was a long pause during which she listened to the static jumping off the troposphere a couple of miles overhead. Finally, he said, "This must be some other Josie Mulkowsky. The one I remember, I knew quite well."

Give the man credit, he was good. With those two little sentences, he cut right through her defenses. He also made her blush, which was no mean feat.

But he had not, and he would not, knock her off balance. Nobody did that to Jocelyn Merriman and the sooner Riordan Nolan found that out, the better for them both.

"It was a long time ago," she said in the gently tolerant voice that nature had designed specifically to frustrate men. No matter what woman said it, in no matter what context, it was the voice of Mother, the all-seeing, all-knowing, and ultimately all-powerful dispenser of cookies, Band-Aids, self-images and—oh, yes, by the way—life itself.

No man—no matter how big, tough, or hardened—was proof against that voice. Some were enraged by it but they were the walking wounded, the scabbed-over, but never really healed survivors of childhood trauma. For most, the voice prompted a quick, protective backpedaling and reassessment.

Exactly as it did with Riordan. He got the message: we aren't going to discuss this. To which he silently amended his own message: at least not right now. Fair enough. He had other things on his mind anyway.

"Got a minute to talk about the scroll?"

"I can probably squeeze it in. Go ahead."

"First, let me say again that this does not represent formal authentication of anything. Without the original, we could be dealing with some grad student's idea of a prank."

"I understand that. With a little luck, the original will be available shortly. In the meantime, what can you tell me?"

"You were right, the writing is Aramaic. Script, syntax, and vocabulary are consistent with the first-century Christian era. As you know, Aramaic was spoken throughout the Middle East but there are particular choices of words here that seem to indicate the writer came from the Palestine area."

Jocelyn took a deep breath and let it out slowly. "Can you tell me anything else about who wrote it?"

"Not much, there isn't enough to go by. But there is a reference to the Sea of Galilee and a visit to the house of a man named Uriel. If it is a forgery, it's very well done."

"How so?"

"Most forgers make a common mistake. Even if they get everything else right, they can't resist the urge to be dramatic. They never write about anything minor like an inventory of somebody's house, or a village census, or in this case a trip to see some guy named Uriel. It's always bigger and glitzier than that. It's like with reincarnation. The past life was always as some Egyptian priestess, never as some poor schmuck rooting around in the mud for something to eat."

Jocelyn flinched slightly. Maybe the fragment Saleem had given her wasn't dramatic, but the claims he was making sure were. Not that she was about to tell Riordan that.

"I get the idea," she said. "So you think this could be on the level?"

"I didn't say that. However, it's worth taking a very close look at the original. In fact, I'd be happy to do it for you. When did you say you expect to have access to it?"

"Soon, I hope," she said. She was feeling cautious all of a sudden. Was it her imagination or was he a bit too willing—not to say eager—to help out? Given his attitude about selling antiquities, she would have expected him to be more reticent.

Certainly, she hadn't thought he'd volunteer to be more involved with a document that, so far as he appeared to know, had no special significance.

Way down in the depths of her mind, Jocelyn was getting some bad vibes. She told herself she was reading too much into nothing but the doubts remained.

"I appreciate your help," she said. "I'll get back in touch with you as soon as I can." Before he could press her any further, if indeed he would have, she got off the phone. She sat for a while, staring unseeingly at the slowly melting ice cream. She was tempted to call Saleem right away but the lateness of the hour stopped her. Instead, she returned to the book she'd been reading.

The Gnostic Gospels were a remarkable collection of documents discovered at the end of 1945 in the northern

Egyptian town of Nag Hammadi. After decades of study, the conclusion was that the writings were by early followers of Jesus who claimed to have secret knowledge of his teachings.

In the struggle to shape the early Christian Church, the gnostics turned out to be the losers. Their writings were banned and they themselves were hunted into extinction. The Nag Hammadi gospels and a handful of other gnostic writings remained the only evidence that such an alternative vision of Christianity had ever existed.

Some of the most important differences between the Gnostic Gospels and the orthodox Christian Bible involved Mary Magdalen. The Bible said little about her beyond acknowledging that she was the first to witness the resurrection. But the gospels went much further.

In them, Mary was described as a close companion of the Messiah's, so much so that others resented her for it. There was even a "Gospel of Mary," one of the few gnostic documents discovered before Nag Hammadi, that went so far as to say that she received special knowledge and visions denied to the other male followers of Jesus.

No doubt about it, Jocelyn thought, Mary Magdalen was—as Wilbur had said—a hot potato so far as traditional Christianity was concerned. People had been trying to push her into the background for almost two thousand years. Yet here she was again, refusing to stay there.

Or at least that was the case if Hassan Saleem was on the level. Big if.

In his apartment a couple of blocks from Columbia University, Riordan also decided against a phone call. His brother's card was on the table beside him. He had only to turn his head slightly to make out the neatly printed numbers where he could be reached in Rome "night or day."

It was day there now. Brendan would be up and about, doing whatever it was he did. If he wasn't immediately reachable, some flunky would know where to find him. He would undoubtedly want to know that just as he'd expected, a first-century Aramaic scroll had turned up. But, so far at least, nobody was making outrageous claims about it.

Certainly not the very circumspect Miss Jocelyn Merriman. He had a feeling that he'd alarmed her, but he wasn't sure how. That wasn't surprising considering that he still didn't have any real idea of what he was dealing with.

He looked again at the photocopy in his hand. The writing was pale and delicate. He tried to picture the person behind it. Not a scribe; a merchant then? A minor official of some sort? Unlikely, since either of those would have had easy recourse to a scribe and been in the habit of using one. Unless there was something controversial about the information that made the writer reluctant to entrust it to anyone else.

He shook his head tiredly. This wasn't getting him anywhere. He needed to get some rest. Tomorrow he'd call Josie again and invent some reason to see her. That wouldn't be hard. She'd changed in a lot of ways. He wanted to know why, and while he was at it he wouldn't mind finding out how much of the sweetly passionate woman he remembered still remained.

Several miles away, at virtually the other end of Manhattan island, Saleem was roused from uneasy sleep. He lay in his bed, listening intently. He could hear a car passing on the street below and farther off, a siren. Closer, he was aware of the dripping on the roof. The rain had stopped but the drains weren't working properly in the old building. Closer still, his heart beat too rapidly.

Somewhere between the dripping water and his heart, he heard the sound that had awakened him, the creak of the old freight elevator rising remorsely upward.

Saleem sprang from the bed. In his long-ago youth he had spent his share of time in the camps in the Bekaa valley, and in them had learned a measure of survival. From the bedside table, he withdrew a Walther .38.

The automatic pistol was his New York gun, as opposed to his Paris gun, his Bahamas gun, and so on. He was never so foolish as to try to move firearms through airport security or customs, preferring instead to simply have them waiting for him at his destination. En route, he relied on a variety of false passports and disguises to give him the anonymity that was his best protection. Now that and every other precaution appeared to have failed him. The creaking grew louder.

Following a routine so thoroughly ingrained in him as to be instinctive, Saleem slipped his feet into the Italian loafers kept beside his bed, and in the same motion picked up the Burberry trench coat left folded over the adjacent chair.

In a pocket of the trench coat was a wallet with one thousand dollars in cash as well as a selection of passports and credit cards. There was a toothbrush as well. Hassan Saleem was a fastidious man.

He was also a prudent one. In his view of the world, survival was always the ultimate victory. Beside that, no number of vanquished enemies counted for anything because there would always be yet another to rise to the challenge.

In other words, it was better to run away and live to see another day.

Without hesitation, Saleem climbed the metal staircase to the roof. He eased open the trapdoor and stepped out. The air was crisp and cool, washed clean of the leaden heaviness of recent days. Despite the ever-present city lights, he thought he could make out a few stars overhead.

He shut the trapdoor quietly behind him and made his way across the roof. Directly next to it was the roof of the adjacent building. The two rooflines were almost on a level, Saleem's building being less than a foot higher than the other. He could climb from one to the other without effort.

In his pocket was a key to the roof door of the other building, purchased the previous year from a cooperative superintendent. The second building also had a conveniently located side exit that gave directly onto an avenue that was busy at any hour of the day or night.

Once there, he could lose himself quickly among the passersby. He would hail a cab or make for the nearest subway station. Within minutes, he could be a mile or more away.

He would not return to the Mulberry Street building. Whether his late-night caller was a random thief or far more, the place was now tainted for him. Not that it mattered. There were always other places for men like him.

As he started to cross the roof, he was pleased to note that his heartbeat had almost returned to normal.

A shadow stepped from behind the small shed that housed the workings for the elevator. Saleem never saw the slender length of wire that, slipped around his throat, quickly and efficiently squeezed the life out of him. His last thought as his knees struck the rain-glistened roof was regret that he had ever heard of the Magdalen Scroll.

7

When Jocelyn couldn't raise Saleem on the phone the following morning from her apartment, she decided to go see him in person. She reached his building in time to see the shiny black body bag being shoved into the ambulance.

A young cop was standing nearby. Jocelyn walked up to him.

"What happened?" she asked, her eyes glued on the back of the ambulance where the foot of the body bag could still be seen. She had a pretty good idea that she already knew the answer but while there was any chance she was wrong, she'd grab it.

The cop scowled. "Move along, miss."

She was a taxpayer, an honest citizen, and genuinely concerned. She stood her ground.

"I'm here to see someone who lives in that building." She pointed in the direction where all the other cops were standing. There was also a bunch of large men in brown business suits of the kind worn only by plain-clothes detectives and some insurance agents. Since insurance seemed kind of superfluous under the circumstances, she bet on the former.

Briefly, she described Saleem. Halfway through, the cop's attitude changed. Far from wanting her to leave, he told her to stay.

"Don't move," he said. "Detective Fairley will want to talk to you."

Fairley was a big, blunt-spoken man, one of the brown suits who had long ago perfected the look of someone who didn't take any crap from anyone. He looked at Jocelyn just long enough to confirm to them both that she was an attractive woman. That done, he turned all business.

"You knew the deceased?"

"That depends," she said, equally cool. The little shiver of apprehension that ran through her was a second cousin to the fear of discovery she had lived with for years. It came from her lower-middle-class background where the police were treated with respect by people who told themselves they had nothing to hide but who always managed to feel obscurely guilty nonetheless.

"I'm here to see Hassan Saleem," she said and ran down the description again.

Detective Fairley nodded. On television, he would have popped out a notebook and started taking notes. In real life, he didn't need to. The stiff had been carrying no less than six IDs, all looking very professionally done and none in the name of Hassan Saleem. One look at them and Fairley had kissed his weekend good-bye. The Feds would be involved before they had the guy on the slab at the chop shop, aka the morgue.

But now here came this very elegant, very cool young

woman who just might represent that Holy Grail of police procedure, A Break in the Case.

"What was the nature of your business with Mr. Saleem?" Detective Fairley asked.

Jocelyn widened her eyes a fraction. "Business? We were just casual acquaintances."

Fairley looked her over again. The year before, he'd gotten involved in a murder case on the Upper East Side that had turned particularly nasty, involving as it did a family that had given the nation a senator, a governor, and two ambassadors, not to mention the publisher of a world-respected newspaper. In the course of it, he'd learned a thing or two about the very rich.

He figured the suit for seven, maybe eight hundred dollars and he wouldn't have been far wrong. It was an Ungaro and it would have run Jocelyn plenty if she hadn't had a friend who got it for her wholesale.

Her job demanded that she dress well and her salary gave her the wherewithal to do so, but the idea of spending as much money as her father had earned in a month on a single article of clothing was more than her Ozone Park soul could stand.

But Detective Fairley couldn't know that. He saw what looked like a rich woman, very much out of place in this part of the lower East Side, much less as an acquaintance, however casual, of anyone who would manage to get himself garroted.

The detective had briefly considered the possibility that this was some new kind of random killing, an exotic variation on the city's endless round of shootings and stabbings. But the thought was so stomach-roiling that he dismissed it out of hand. No, the answer lay in Mr. Six

Identities, aka Hassan Saleem, and the very classy lady standing in front of him just might know it.

At the same time that all this was going through the mind of Detective Fairley, Jocelyn was thinking fast. Saleem was dead and there were too many brown suits hanging around to make it look like natural causes. She'd done her civic duty by giving them his name. She wasn't about to start explaining about the Magdalen Scroll or anything related to it.

Already out of the corner of her eye, she could see the first television truck pulling up. Time to go.

For once, luck favored her. One of the uniformed policemen called Detective Fairley over to check out something he'd found in a garbage can in front of the building. While the detective's back was turned, Jocelyn made her move.

She slipped away with a skill Saleem would have admired had he still been in any condition to do so. But unlike him, her heart was beating unnaturally fast. By the time she reached the avenue, her knees felt weak.

She grabbed the first cab that happened by and was about to give the driver Holcroft & Farnsworth's address when she thought better of it. She had him let her out ten blocks from the office and walked the rest of the way. If Detective Fairley tried to track down the woman he'd been talking with he might be able to locate the cabbie, but he wouldn't get much farther than that.

Trey was sufficiently recovered to be back at his post. He gave her a startled glance as she came in.

"You look awful," he said. "What's the matter?"

"I had a deal killed on me."

He winced. "Too bad. Want me to make tea?"

"Sure, sure, whatever." Make tea, type a letter, anything so long as he got out of her hair. She needed to think fast.

Except there really wasn't anything to think about. Saleem was dead and with that any route to the Magdalen Scroll seemed firmly closed off. She had no idea where to even start looking, presuming there actually was something to look for.

And then there was the little matter of the killing. Maybe it hadn't been related to the scroll at all; who knew what else Saleem had been involved with. On the other hand, maybe she should just forget the whole thing.

There was a note on her desk that Wilbur wanted to see her. Trey pointed it out when he returned with the tea. He also had the mail. Most of it he had opened and neatly sorted into three piles. One required her immediate attention and was thankfully slim, the second could wait, and the third was in neither of the first two because it was marked "Personal and Confidential."

It consisted of a single letter in a standard white business envelope. Her address was neatly typed. There was no return address.

Jocelyn took a sip of her tea and opened the envelope. Inside was a sheet of plain bond paper folded once down the middle. The date on the top of the paper was the previous day's. The short message had been typed.

"Miss Merriman," the message read, "The fourth caliph of Islam, successor of the Prophet, was his son-in-law, Alī ibn Abī Tālib, also known as the Lion of God. He wrote a wise book called *A Hundred Sayings* which you might enjoy studying some time. One of the sayings is this: He who has a thousand friends has not a friend to spare, And he who has one enemy will meet him everywhere.

"I fear the time of meeting may be upon me. Should

anything unfortunate occur, go to San Crisogono and seek there the one called Jamal.

"God is the Light of the Heavens and of the Earth. His Light is like a niche in which is a lamp—the lamp encased in glass—the glass, as it were, a glistening star. From a blessed tree is it lighted, the olive neither from the East nor of the West, whose oil would well nigh shine out, even though fire touched it not. It is light upon light. God guideth whom He will to His light, and God setteth forth parables to men, for God knoweth all things."

The note ended in a scrawl of black ink and the name— Hassan Saleem.

Jocelyn exhaled slowly. Her eyes were damp. She had barely known Hassan while he was alive but now, too late, he was sharply clarified in her mind. Whatever else he had been, he was a man of learning and a man of faith.

She recognized the last quote regarding the light of God as being from the Koran. Perhaps it had brought comfort to Hassan in his final hours. Or perhaps it was intended as something more.

Seek Jamal at San Crisogono. The reference was sufficiently cryptic to confuse most people but it was clear enough to Jocelyn, as Hassan had undoubtedly believed it would be. Anyone with any pretension to expertise in antiquities, particularly someone like her who had studied in Italy, would know the old church of St. Crysogonos, called San Crisogono, in the Trastevere neighborhood of Rome.

The church was renowned for its eighth- and tenth-century murals. Jocelyn had visited it as a student. She still remembered the shivery sense of fear and anticipation that came with the descent deep underground, far from the bustle of modern Rome, into a place of cool silence and millennium-old reverence.

With a quote from the fourth caliph and a possible clue from the Koran, Hassan had sent her into an ancient Christian church in search of the testament of the woman who had followed an itinerant Jewish rabbi into death and beyond.

Was it any wonder she liked her job?

She folded the note carefully, put it back in the envelope, and slipped both into the slit pocket of her skirt. That left Wilbur's note sitting on her desk: See me ASAP. It wasn't like Wilbur to be so curt. When he communicated at all with his employees, it was in obscure asides usually murmured over sherry and biscuits. But not this time.

He was in his office when she got there. "Sit down," he said pleasantly, gesturing to the guest chair opposite his desk. "I've been concerned about your meeting with the Arab gentleman, what was his name?"

"Hassan Saleem," Jocelyn said. She hesitated. Wilbur was her friend as well as her employer. He was also an elderly man with an uncertain heart. She didn't like the idea of distressing him, but she had a duty to keep him informed.

"Mr. Saleem is dead," she said quietly. "His body was found this morning. Apparently, he was murdered."

A flush of color spread over Wilbur's baby-smooth cheeks as far as the shiny dome of his head. His hands on the desk in front of him shook slightly. "I see," he murmured. "Most unfortunate. I take it this ends the matter?"

"Not entirely. Before he died, Mr. Saleem gave me a photocopy of what he claimed to be a portion of the scroll. I showed it to Professor Riordan Nolan at Columbia who has confirmed that it is first-century Aramaic and probably from the Palestine area. Of course, the possibility exists that it is still a forgery, but with that much to go on I really want to proceed."

Wilbur raised his eyebrows quizzically. "How can you?"

Jocelyn hesitated. It had suddenly occurred to her that Wilbur had known of her meeting with Saleem, had even known the address she was going to. The idea that he could have had anything to do with Saleem's death was absurd, and yet with so much at stake her instincts were telling her to go cautiously.

"Before he died," she said, "Mr. Saleem sent me a note telling me who to contact in Rome."

Wilbur's face stiffened. "Indeed? How thoughtful of him. Who did he say?"

"A man named Jamal at . . ." There it was again, the faint urging deep down inside her that this was not the time to tell everything she knew. Yet there was Wilbur, eyes watchful, waiting for her.

She took a breath and said, "at the church of San Constanza."

San Constanza was yet another of the centuries-old churches that dotted Rome. But it lay far removed from the Trastevere in the so-called African district named for the conquests of the Mussolini era.

Like San Crisogono, it was noted for its ancient artwork, in its case mosaics, but it did not, so far as Jocelyn knew, have any link to anyone named Jamal.

If questioned later, she could always say that the two churches—San Constanza and San Crisogono—sounded sufficiently alike for Wilbur to have heard her incorrectly. It was a slim cover and a worse lie. She felt uncomfortable and for a moment was tempted to tell him the truth. But the memory of the black body bag sliding into the ambulance stopped her.

Instead, she said, "I can leave for Rome tonight."

Wilbur nodded thoughtfully. "Very well, but I insist you be careful. Keep in touch with me and if you have any sense of danger, get out immediately. Nothing is worth risking another death."

Jocelyn agreed with him wholeheartedly. She went back to her office a short time later and told Trey where she was going. While he booked her flight and hotel, she sorted through whatever couldn't wait until later.

That done she thought about calling Riordan. He had said he wanted to remain involved, but she was reluctant. It was almost too tempting to turn to him for help. Her susceptibility to him surprised and frightened her. She didn't like feeling so vulnerable.

Yet she liked even less the thought of walking into a potentially bad situation on her own.

She finished everything she needed to and was ready to leave when she paused. Before she could think about it any more, she reached for the phone. It rang several times before a woman answered.

She was the department secretary. Professor Nolan was teaching and would be tied up the remainder of the day. Would she care to leave a message?

Briefly, Jocelyn identified herself, explained where she was going and left the name of her hotel in Rome. If he wanted to get in touch with her, he could. And if he didn't, she would manage fine on her own.

She went home to pack. Two hours later she was at the airport. Twilight was falling over the city as the Air Italia jet lifted off.

Jocelyn settled back in her first-class seat, shut her eyes, and thought about Hassan. She had not prayed in years and she did not do so now, at least not in any way she thought of as praying.

But she did remember the words of the Koran—God guideth whom He will to His light—and hoped that for Hassan the journey had proved worthwhile.

8

Jocelyn was booked into the Grand Hotel off the Via Veneto. Left to her own devices, she would have preferred something simpler and more private. But Wilbur always stayed at the Grand back when he was traveling the world on behalf of the firm, and he insisted that his top employees continue the tradition.

So the Grand it was. She was whisked through registration with efficiency she didn't always associate with Rome, or anywhere else for that matter, and shown upstairs to one of the gracious blue and pale gold bedrooms complete with crystal chandelier, marble bath, and all the other accoutrements common to such places.

There had been a time when Jocelyn was thrilled by such opulence—what girl from Ozone Park wouldn't be? But the thrill was long since gone. She hardly noticed it as she tipped the bellboy, kicked her shoes off, and flopped down on the king-size bed.

No matter how much traveling she did, she never managed to get around the problem of jet lag. All the usual strategies—no alcohol, plenty of other fluids, catnapping, etc.—failed her.

She finished every trans-Atlantic trip worn out, fuzzy, and with a disconcerting sense of being in two places at the same time, part of her still on New York time and the rest struggling to cope with wherever she had landed herself.

The only solution she'd ever found was to not fight it. She got up, took off her clothes, and put them away neatly in the closet. Wrapped in a favorite old cotton nightie, she pulled the covers back and got into the bed. Her head touched the cool, smooth pillow. Moments later she was asleep.

When she awoke, it was late afternoon. She could hear the sound of traffic outside her windows and the muted rattle of a room service cart in the corridor. For a moment, she had no idea where she was. Then her eyes fell on the blue-and-gold carpet and she remembered.

She rose and went into the bathroom. The huge tub was tempting but she settled for a shower instead. Refreshed, she dressed in slacks, a silk blouse, and a suede jacket. Before she left the room, she checked to make sure the note from Hassan was in her purse.

The Grand was justly famous for its afternoon tea. The main bar was filled with elegantly dressed men and women sipping their Earl Grey and downing elaborate pastries. Jocelyn's stomach growled but she ignored it. She'd eat later after she'd taken care of business.

She got a taxi outside the hotel and directed the driver to a street on the same side of the river. From there, she walked across the Ponte Garibaldi into the Trastevere district.

Being on the far side of the Tiber, the area had begun

life independent of the Roman colossus and still retained much of its unique character. The maze of narrow streets had their share of trendy boutiques but the old flavor of neighborhood grocery stores, wine shops, and artisans' studios remained.

In late afternoon, the sidewalks were aswarm with shoppers returning home from work, weary tourists wringing the last full measure from the day, and black-clad grandmothers sitting on their stoops to observe the passing scene. Mopeds zipped through the winding streets, coming within a hair's breadth of disaster at every turn but continuing blithely on their way.

San Crisogono was only a few blocks from the river. Jocelyn found it without difficulty. She remembered the simple, stone structure well enough.

The basilica was empty. Light flowing through the great windows of the nave illuminated stucco pillars and a coffered ceiling emblazoned with the arms of Cardinal Borghese. They were embellishments added to the church during one of its several updatings, but the overall effect was still medieval.

Despite the warmth of the day, Jocelyn shivered slightly. There was a chill to the old stones that no amount of sunlight could ease.

It was her hope that she would find the sacristan somewhere about, but he was not on hand. There was only a tiny, black-robed nun down on her knees scrubbing the stone floor. She looked up startled when Jocelyn approached.

Speaking softly, so as not to alarm her further, Jocelyn apologized for intruding on her work. The nun was very old with a seamed face and gnarled hands. She blinked once, twice, at the apparition before her and went back to her scrubbing.

"I am looking for someone named Jamal," Jocelyn said in Italian. "Do you know of such a person?"

The scrubbing continued without pause, swoosh-swoosh across the floor Jocelyn knew to have been laid down in the thirteenth century. How many legions of reverent nuns had scrubbed it since then? How many callused knees and reddened hands, how many oceans of water and soap? All to the greater glory of God.

"Why do you seek him?" the nun asked without looking up again.

"I . . . I have a message for him," Jocelyn said. It was true in a sense. Whoever Jamal might be, it was likely he would want to know of Hassan's death.

"Not here."

"There is no one named Jamal?" Disappointment flooded through her. If that proved true, she really was at a dead end.

The nun shook her head. "Not since Tuesday. He comes to work then, says he doesn't feel well, and that's the last anyone sees of him. Who knows where he is now?"

The way she said it suggested that the less pleasant the destination, the more likely it was he was there.

"Oh, I see." Hope surged again. "Do you know where he lives?"

The nun shrugged. She dumped the scrub brush back into the pail, shook the excess water off it, and slapped it down again on the marble.

"Somewhere. He's a bad one, I know that. Claiming to be a good Catholic so he could get the job here, but not once going to confession or even lighting a candle."

Her voice dropped, becoming fraught with significance. "He's an infidel, if you ask me, and no loss. Good riddance to him."

Having neatly consigned the missing Jamal to the netherworld of nonbelievers, the nun returned her full attention to her task. Jocelyn was left to make her way out of the church. She stood in the stark sunlight, blinking, and trying to decide what to do next.

Jamal had worked at San Crisogono, of that much she was now sure. He could have come to the church from any of the lower-class neighborhoods in and around Rome, but it was more likely that he would have sought work as close to home as possible. If she was to have any chance of finding him, she had to hope that was the case.

In the teeming streets of the Trastevere, the task seemed impossible. She dodged a moped, ignored the suggestion of the young man riding it, and found a seat on the sidewalk in front of a small trattoria. The waiter who brought her a San Pellegrino was friendly and had little else to occupy him at the moment. He had no hesitation about replying to the questions of the lovely American lady who spoke such unusually fine Italian.

Yes, indeed, there were Arabs living in the neighborhood, quite a few as a matter of fact. Good people for the most part, like everybody else. It wasn't true that the Trastevere had fallen prey to pickpockets and purse snatchers, and that the tourists were no longer safe there. Not true at all. He didn't know anyone named Jamal himself but he did know a man who had a stall on the Via Gloriso and who was from Egypt originally. He might know this Jamal person.

Jocelyn paused barely long enough to thank the waiter, finish her mineral water, and leave a substantial tip. She was crossing a side street not far from the trattoria when a low, black limousine suddenly shot out directly in front of her. The car was traveling at a very high rate of speed.

Jocelyn had a vivid, slow-motion impression of the roar of the powerful engine, the smell of exhaust, and a brief glimpse of a black-clad driver behind the wheel, bearing down on her without a flicker of expression. It was all she could do to jump out of the way an instant before she would have been crushed beneath the wheels. As it was, the car sideswiped her and she fell hard against the pavement.

By the time she managed to rise again, a small crowd had gathered. People stood around shaking their heads and talking about how you took your life in your hands these days to go outside for a liter of wine. Cars continued to rush past on the busy street, horns honked, drivers shouted, but of the limousine itself there was no sign. It had vanished as thoroughly as though it had never been.

Jocelyn declined the offer of help from several people and limped back to the trattoria where the waiter, after recovering from his shock that such a thing should happen to such a nice young lady, called for a cab. The Egyptian would have to wait. One of Jocelyn's legs was badly scraped, her right arm throbbed, and she felt as though she had managed to bruise a rib. All she wanted to do was get back to the hotel and assess the damage.

She was walking slowly into the lobby, hoping not to attract too much attention, when a movement near the reception desk caught her eye. There was a man standing there, dressed in jeans, an old blue dress shirt, and a tweed jacket. He had a single, battered suitcase at his feet.

The desk clerk looked slightly bemused but the man's

obvious assurance carried more weight than his somewhat unorthodox appearance. At the Grand, they were well-accustomed to the notion that the wealthy, the powerful, and the influential sometimes showed up in unusual guises.

The man turned and Jocelyn saw his face. She should have been surprised but all she felt instead was relief. Hobbling slightly, she went over to the desk.

"Hello, Riordan," she said and because she couldn't help it, she smiled.

9

Riordan scowled. "What the hell happened to you?"

"I fell," Jocelyn said. She took his arm and gave the desk clerk a quick, reassuring nod. "I've got a lot to tell you. Let's go sit down somewhere."

The somewhere she had in mind was her room. By the time Riordan realized that he was past being surprised. Ever since getting her message he'd been in perpetual motion, arranging for his classes to be covered and getting that idiot who worked for her to say where she'd gone.

As was his custom, he'd slept almost all the way across the Atlantic and arrived in Rome refreshed. He was ready for just about anything, but not for the sight of a bruised and battered Jocelyn with her auburn hair tumbling around her shoulders and shadows under her brown-gold eyes.

He dropped his bag on the floor right inside the room, shut the door, and scowled again. "I'm going to ask you one more time, what happened?"

"I had a close encounter with a stretch limo," she said. "It's not a big deal."

Except that just the effort it took to stand was starting to cost her. She winced and hoped he didn't see it.

"I'm going to get cleaned up. While I do that, would you mind ordering some dinner? I'm starved."

"We could go out," he suggested.

"I'm not up to it. Room service will be fine." She disappeared into the bathroom. A moment later, he heard the water running in the tub.

Riordan walked over to the ornate desk and fished around in the drawer until he found the leather-covered room service menu. He told himself she was merely being practical. She was tired, he could see that, and she'd had a scare. Naturally, she wanted to take it easy.

The fact that she was treating him like a casual friend instead of like a man she'd had a brief but—so far as he recalled—very intense affair with didn't matter at all.

Right.

He ran his eye down the menu, picked out what looked good, and phoned the order in. That done, he went over to the bathroom door and called through it. "Everything okay?"

"Fine. I was lucky." She had to keep reminding herself of that. Her right calf was scraped from the ankle to the knee, her elbow on the same side was stiffening up, and she had a nasty bruise near her ribs. So far as she could tell, she didn't need a doctor but it had been a close call.

"Accidents happen," she said as she came out of the bathroom. Her hair was wrapped turban-style in a towel and the rest of her was swallowed up by the oversized terry cloth robe the hotel provided.

"Was this one?" Riordan asked. He wasn't going to

think about how good she looked despite what she'd just been through.

He scanned her face, noting that she'd been right, the little bump was still there on the bridge of her nose. It kept her from being classically perfect but that was only to the good. She looked beautiful, warm, intelligent, and thoroughly feminine. He was glad he'd come.

"What else could it have been?" Jocelyn asked. She sat down on the edge of the bed. "You know how traffic is here."

"Where were you exactly?"

If she was ever going to lay it out for him, it had to be now. And if she wasn't going to, then she'd had no business suggesting they talk in her room. Either they had something to talk about or they—

She didn't complete the thought. Other things she and Riordan could do were simply not on the schedule. At least, not if she had any sense.

"I was in the Trastevere district," she said. "I went there to follow up on a lead I got about the possible location of the Magdalen Scroll."

"From the client in New York?"

She nodded and was about to go on when the rattle of the room service cart stopped her. Riordan opened the door for the waiter. Minutes later, their dinner was served and they were alone again.

Riordan held her chair for her as she sat, then took his own on the other side of the table. He smiled. "You look very fetching."

Jocelyn laughed. "That's one of the things I like most about room service. Most restaurants won't let you dine in your bathrobe."

He caught the little flinch that accompanied her laughter and said, "You really aren't feeling well, are you?"

"I've been better," she admitted. "But I'm sure by morning the worst will be over. Anyway, we were talking about the client."

She took a breath, looked at him directly, and said, "I'm not completely sure what all is involved here, but I am convinced I need help. Unless you want to bow out now, you're it."

"I'm in," he said bluntly. "Now suppose you tell me what's going on."

"The client was a man named Hassan Saleem. He was murdered yesterday in New York."

"I thought the name sounded familiar," Riordan said. "It was on the news right before I left." His face tightened. "He was garroted."

"I didn't know that," Jocelyn said quietly. The food in front of her was delectable but she was losing her appetite.

"He contacted me four days ago and said he had an important artifact to sell. I went to see him. He was very security conscious. He claimed the original was too valuable to risk moving on his own but he was also worried about his personal safety. Maybe he had a premonition or an actual warning, but shortly before he died, he mailed this letter to me."

She reached over to the desk where she had left her purse and withdrew the note from Saleem. Riordan scanned it quickly.

"Interesting," he said. "So you went to San Crisogono?"

Jocelyn nodded. "It turns out there was a Jamal working there but he hasn't been around since Tuesday. I was trying to find him when I had my little mishap."

"Okay, it's clear enough so far. But you haven't told me what Saleem claimed to be selling."

"That's where it gets crazy. He said he had the Magdalen Scroll."

Riordan took a sip of the lightly sparkling white wine he had ordered and looked at her over the rim of the glass. "And you believed him?"

"Of course not. But I wasn't ready to completely disbelieve him either, especially not after what you confirmed about the photocopy. I thought if there was any chance, no matter how remote, that he was on the level, I should at least spend some time checking it out."

Riordan sat back in his chair. He had the sense that she was being absolutely straight with him and that it was a good thing. They were going to have to be able to trust each other, at least up to a point.

"Four days ago?" he asked.

Jocelyn nodded. "That's right. It's hard to believe how much has happened since then."

More than she knew, but he wasn't going to get into that. This was no time to mention Brendan.

"You realize," he said, "there is absolutely no basis for believing there is any such thing as the Magdalen Scroll?"

"Then why have people been talking about it for so many centuries? If there was nothing whatsoever to the legend, it would have died out by now."

"Maybe," Riordan said, "but if the Magdalen Scroll actually exists—and if it really is the testament of Mary Magdalen—why would the Vatican keep it hidden?"

"You know the answer to that as well as I do. Because it

contains information—teachings, if you will—that challenge Church doctrine."

"Then why didn't they destroy it?" Riordan asked.

"I don't know," Jocelyn admitted. She had to agree that would have been a likelier course. The Gnostic writings would never have survived if they hadn't been buried at Nag Hammadi. Even then there was no telling how many others had been burned, their authors executed for daring to differ from the orthodox view.

"I'm not claiming to have all the answers," she said. "I just want a chance to ask the right questions. To start with, I want to find Jamal."

"But not on your own. I'm staying."

"Fine. We can call down and get you a room—"

"I'm staying here." Before she could say anything, he went on, "There's already been one murder. I'm not taking any chances on there being another. We're both adults. There shouldn't be any problem with us sharing a room for a few days."

His eyebrows rose slightly. "Should there?"

"No, of course not," Jocelyn said quickly. Much as she hated to admit it, the thought of having him so near made her feel safe and protected. It also made her feel other ways, too, but she wasn't going to think about that.

"You're right," she said, "that's probably the most sensible course."

"Tomorrow, we'll look for Jamal. But for the moment, you ought to get some rest."

Jocelyn agreed. They finished dinner a short time later. Riordan wheeled the cart back outside while she turned down the bed. She was so tired by then that she could barely see straight.

When he put an arm around her gently and eased her

under the covers, she offered no objection. For the first time in a very long time, she was content to let somebody else make the decisions. That wouldn't last, but while it did she might as well enjoy it.

Riordan switched off all but one of the lights. He sat down in the chair across from the bed with the last of the wine beside him. When he was sure Jocelyn was asleep, he took a book out of his bag and settled down to read.

It was a small volume, covered in cracked leather with the pages frayed around the edges. Printed in Venice in 1537, it was one of only four known surviving copies. He had been extremely lucky to find it.

He settled himself more comfortably in his chair and took a sip of the wine. The rest remained forgotten beside him as he began to read. The small book was the diary of one Lorenzo di Costello, a twelfth-century merchant and traveler, published long after his death. It held Riordan's attention well into the night.

10

The next morning, they set out to find Jamal. Riordan suggested starting back at the church again on the chance that he might have turned up. He hadn't.

They went on from there to the Via Gloriso. They were early, the stalls and barrows were only just being uncovered, their owners sipping thick black coffee in the morning sun and chatting lazily.

They found the Egyptian without difficulty. He was a tall, slender man who ran a stall filled with brightly colored beaded and spangled fabrics set on poles to flutter in the spring breeze. A gaily painted sign gave a name to his business—MA DONNA.

On the wall of the building behind the stall was one of the many stone madonnas common to the district. Streaked with soot and eroded by acid rain, it nonetheless possessed a certain restrained beauty.

Riordan startled the Egyptian by introducing Jocelyn and himself in fluent Arabic and complimenting him on the worthiness of his goods. After his initial surprise, the man grinned and launched into a speech of his own about the excellence of Riordan's Arabic, the loveliness of his companion, and the great good fortune that had brought them together on this particularly promising day.

Riordan agreed as to how that was the case and suggested that the white diaphanous silk would look very good on Jocelyn. The Egyptian—whose name was Ahmed ben Ibraheim—demurred politely and suggested the rose-colored silk would actually be more appropriate to her coloring.

Jocelyn understood little of their exchange except what she could make out from their gestures and their general masculine bonhomie. She swallowed her impatience, admired the rose, and suggested one or two of the little gold bangles ben Ibraheim also sold would go nicely with it.

That left the matter of price. Riordan enjoyed haggling and was good at it; Ahmed enjoyed the rarity of having someone with whom to match wits. They could have gone on at length and would have had not Jocelyn begun shifting from one foot to the other and staring off pointedly into space.

The two men exchanged a final glance of masculine understanding and completed the transaction. As Ahmed was wrapping the fabric, Riordan counted the money from his wallet.

Handing it over, he said, "Given the excellence of your location and the obviously superior nature of your goods, it is likely you are a man of standing in these parts, is it not?"

Ahmed smiled modestly. "There are some who say so."

"I wonder if you might be able to help the lady. She is looking for a friend of a friend for whom she has a message. Alas, she has little information about where he might be found and she is concerned that she may have to return home without speaking to him."

Ahmed sighed and spread his hands in regret. "Rome is a very large place. Naturally, I would help if I could but—"

"The person in question is Arab. He used to work at the church of San Crisogono but he has not been there recently. His name is Jamal. Perhaps you know of him?"

Ahmed looked from one of them to the other. His large, almond-shaped eyes narrowed. "You say he is a friend of the lady?"

"A friend of her friend. She has come all the way from New York and she is most anxious to speak with him."

"Then the friend should have given her this Jamal person's address or at the very least the number at which to telephone him. Most irresponsible not to, wouldn't you say?"

"Alas, the friend was indisposed at the time. He said only that she would find Jamal at San Crisogono. But he is not there."

"I see," Ahmed murmured. Again, he scrutinized them both. "The matter is urgent?"

"It could be viewed in that light."

"How unfortunate then that I do not know of him."

"Indeed," Riordan said with regret. He withdrew his wallet again.

Ahmed stiffened. "It is not a matter for—" he began.

"Of course not," Riordan said quickly, dismissing any notion that it would be necessary to bribe so eminent and upstanding a man.

Certain Westerners might be subject to such misapprehension but he, having studied the enlightened ways of Islam, understood when such things were and were not done. He took a business card from his wallet and jotted a number on the back before handing it to Ahmed.

"If by any chance you should encounter such a person, unlikely as that is, perhaps you would be kind enough to give him this. We are staying at the Grand."

Ahmed studied the card. He nodded thoughtfully. "You are a scholar."

"I have some poor ability."

"I am certain your students praise your name. What is your field?"

"The study of antiquities. They are also the field of this lady, Miss Jocelyn Merriman."

Jocelyn could make out her own name and saw the flash of interest on the man's face. But Ahmed said nothing more. He merely pocketed the card and bowed his farewells.

As they were walking away, Riordan carrying the package, Jocelyn said, "What do we do now? We can't go through the whole Trastevere asking anyone who looks Arab if they know somebody named Jamal."

"We don't need to. Ben Ibraheim knows him."

Jocelyn looked at him quickly. "He said he didn't."

"Of course. He doesn't yet know whether Jamal wants anything to do with us so he would naturally be discreet. But he'll pass the message along."

"I don't see how you can be so sure."

"He didn't want any money." When she continued to look doubtful, Riordan explained. "If he genuinely didn't know Jamal and was merely going to hold onto my card on the off chance he might happen to encounter him, he would have expected at least some small payment for that service. If he preferred not to be involved in any way, he wouldn't take either the card or the money. Taking the card alone means he knows Jamal and, further, he has some sense of concern for him or perhaps he feels superior to him in some way. Both would prevent him from accepting payment for passing along the message. It's simple really."

"Maybe to you," Jocelyn said skeptically.

Riordan laughed. "I've spent a lot of time in the Middle East. After a while, you get a feel for how things are done."

She had little choice but to believe him. "What do we do now? Go back to the hotel and wait?"

"There's not much point. Ben Ibraheim can't leave his stall unattended. It will probably be at least a few hours before the message is passed along and then Jamal has to decide what he wants to do. I've only been in Rome a couple of times. How about you show me the high points?"

Jocelyn was willing enough. Rome was one of her favorite cities and she never tired of exploring it. By common consent, they settled on the oldest part of the city, the Palatine hill with its pleasant walks amid flower beds, shady trees, and overgrown ruins.

They began, appropriately enough, at the oldest and in many ways most remarkable site, the remains of several small huts dating from the time of the city's founding. From there they moved on through the roofless palaces that had housed emperors of the world to the temples where they had worshipped. Most interesting of these, at least to Jocelyn, was the Temple of Cybele, raised to honor the Mother Goddess whose worship flowered in Rome a few centuries before the coming of Christianity.

By the time they had seen all they wanted to, it was getting on for lunch. They went to the nearby "Vecchia

Roma" where they sat outside under the white umbrellas. Over freshwater shrimp and grilled chicken, Riordan said, "You look better than yesterday. No ill effects?"

She shook her head. "My elbow still twinges every once in a while but that's it. I still think it was an accident."

"Maybe, maybe not. I've been doing some more thinking about the Magdalen Scroll. I'm still not convinced it exists, but let's presume for the moment that it might. If there is such a document, there's at least a possibility that it could have ended up in the Vatican archives."

Jocelyn put down her fork and looked at him. "What makes you say that?"

"Have you ever heard of a man named Lorenzo di Costello?"

Jocelyn shook her head. "I don't think so."

"There's no reason you should have, he's pretty obscure. He was the second or maybe the third son of a Venetian merchant family back in the eleventh—twelfth —century. He did a fair amount of traveling and he got into a few tight spots, but the most interesting thing about him is that he kept a diary. Toward the end of 1099, he managed to land himself in Jerusalem right after it fell to the Crusaders."

"Probably not the best place to be at the time," Jocelyn said.

"Probably not," Riordan agreed. "It was your typical conquered city—burning buildings, streets full of bodies, people running around screaming, and lots of looting. It was the looting that interested Lorenzo in particular."

"I suppose he did his share?"

"Possibly, he didn't say. What he did write in his diary was the fate that befell a prosperous Palestinian family, the Khalduns, who had lived in Jerusalem for generations. It concerned him because he actually knew the Khalduns through his own family's trading contacts. The Khalduns had an extensive private library that included some very rare old scrolls. Di Costello says that immediately after the fall of Jerusalem, the library was seized by a group of papal knights. In the process, all the Khalduns were killed except for a single son whom Lorenzo claimed he saved. He makes some other interesting claims too."

"Such as?"

"Among other things, he says it was no accident that the Khalduns were robbed and killed. According to him, they were personally targeted at the direct order of a papal representative who was along on the Crusade. Further, he says that the documents taken from them were early church writings written in the language of the Lord Jesus himself, which would have been Aramaic and—get this—he says there was also what he refers to as 'that which may not be spoken of but which is holiest among holy.'"

"What's that supposed to mean?" Jocelyn asked, frowning.

"I have no idea. The point is, di Costello's is the only eyewitness account of a group of early church documents written in Aramaic coming into the hands of the Vatican. He says they were all sent back to Rome under guard. Now maybe this has nothing at all to do with Saleem or any supposed Magdalen Scroll, but the really interesting thing is what happened later. Lorenzo went home, lived another forty years, had eight kids, and ended up head of the family. After he died, his diary was preserved in the di Costellos' own archives. Finally, in the 1500s, somebody in the family got the idea to publish it. Several dozen copies were printed but they were almost immediately confiscated and suppressed *at the direct order of the Vatican*. Only four copies survived, one of which happened to end up in the hands of a colleague of mine who was kind enough to let me borrow it."

"You mean you actually have it here?" Jocelyn asked.

Riordan nodded. "You can read it for yourself. What do you say we head back to the hotel?"

Jocelyn agreed immediately. A faint suspicion was beginning to grow in her mind, one so strange that she could hardly credit it. Yet it remained, refusing to be dismissed, whispering of ancient crimes and long-delayed revenge.

11

Jocelyn read the di Costello diary seated at the desk in her room at the Grand. The small book comprised several hundred pages of which about fifty dealt with the events in Jerusalem at the end of 1099. She read them slowly, taking great care to understand the vulgate Latin in which they were written.

Riordan, who had been up far into the night with the diary, stretched out on the bed and dozed. From time to time, Jocelyn looked at him. He lay on his back with his head to one side, a lock of his thick black hair falling across his forehead. There was a nick on his chin where he'd cut himself shaving that morning.

He'd risen early while she was still deeply asleep and had been finished in the bathroom before she awoke. He left it tidy but there was an unmistakable sense of intimacy in the jumbling of his shaving brush and soap with her face cream and makeup, his towels next to hers, the second, larger terry cloth robe the hotel had sent up added to the one she was using.

The small domestic details bewildered Jocelyn. She had known him so briefly, if explosively, and he had come back into her life so suddenly. Yet here he was, looking settled and comfortable, as though they had been together all this time, an old married couple embarked on companionable adventure.

It made no sense that he could slide so easily into a niche in her life that she hadn't even been aware was empty. Yet there was no denying that with him she felt stronger, safer, and just plain happier despite everything else that was happening.

She put down the diary and sighed softly. No doubt about it, life could be flat-out peculiar at times.

Riordan heard the sigh. It reached him through dreams that were light and fragile. He opened his eyes. Jocelyn was watching him. There was a look on her face he didn't need explained.

As though he had just been thinking about it, he said, "I asked you to come with me."

She nodded. "I know, but Anatolia was so far away and we had only known each other a few days. And then I did have my own studies. Believe me, I was tempted but it just seemed like too much of a risk."

"I was asking a lot of you," he acknowledged. "And maybe you were right, maybe it wouldn't have worked out. You've done a great deal with your life."

She smiled faintly. "That's a surprise coming from you. I thought you thoroughly disapproved of institutions like Holcroft & Farnsworth."

"Not thoroughly, only mainly. I'm willing to admit there are good people working in such places. You're one of them."

He smiled in turn. "Whoever you are, Josie Mulkow-sky/Jocelyn Merriman, you're a hell of a lady."

The roughly tender compliment made her eyes sting. She blinked and looked away. "You're not so bad your-self."

He laughed, a low rumbling sound that shot straight through her. "Face it, we're a couple of romantics. How about coming over here?"

"Over there?"

"Yes."

"Well . . . I suppose I could."

He held out a hand.

She got up slowly and walked across the room. It wasn't far, less than a dozen steps, but it seemed a great distance. Not until his fingers closed around hers did she feel she had made it safely.

"That wasn't so hard, was it?" he asked.

She shook her head. "I guess not." She felt awkward standing next to the bed. When he tugged gently, she sat.

His legs were pressed against her side, his hand still held hers, she could feel the warmth and strength ema-nating from him. A dizzying sensation crept over her. The world beyond the quiet room seemed to grow more dis-tant. From one heartbeat to the next, she felt herself on an edge, peering over, trying to see what might be beyond in the instant before she tumbled into it.

"Riordan . . ."

The phone rang.

He uttered a particularly blunt expletive and reached for the receiver.

Jocelyn waited as he listened. When he replied, it was in Arabic. After several moments and a bit more conversa-tion, he put the phone down and shook his head wryly.

"That was ben Ibraheim. He apologizes for disturbing us in the midst of our scholarly endeavors but says that on a day this pleasant, we might wish to stroll along the river near the Villa Farnesina."

Jocelyn drew an unsteady breath. The transition back to a larger reality was not easy. "We might?"

"So says friend ben Ibraheim."

"Does he say when?"

"I gather now would be a good time."

It was just as well, Jocelyn told herself as they rode down in the elevator. She had enough to be concerned about without plunging into a relationship she wasn't sure was a good idea to start with. It had been hard enough to get over Riordan the first time around; she certainly didn't want to go through that again. Ben Ibraheim might very well have saved her from a bad mistake.

None of which soothed her unsettled emotions. There was an ache deep inside her that no amount of reason could cure. Worse yet, she was in danger of getting used to it.

She was glad when they were back out in the sunshine and headed once more across the river to the sixteenth-century villa close to the banks of the Tiber and only a short distance from the Trastevere.

By then it was late afternoon. Most of the tourists had gone back to their hotels to rest before venturing out for the evening and the Romans themselves were still at work, with the result that the paved walkway that ran between the river and the villa's sumptuous gardens was almost empty.

They found a place to sit on a wrought-iron bench and waited. Ten minutes passed, then fifteen. When almost twenty had gone by, Riordan said, "This may not be getting us anywhere."

Jocelyn laid a hand on his arm. "Wait," she said. "I've got a feeling."

She had noticed a slender, dark-eyed boy who three times had bicycled past them, always appearing to take no notice of the couple sitting on the bench yet still managing to give the impression that he missed nothing. She could see him coming in their direction again.

As he neared, Jocelyn raised her voice and said in clear Italian, "I don't think we should give up yet. Mr. ben Ibraheim said to come here."

Riordan realized what she was doing and looked around quickly. He saw the boy. He had stopped his bicycle and stood with one foot on the ground, the other poised as though for a quick getaway should that prove necessary.

From the distance of several yards that separated them, he said, "Are you the ones looking for Jamal?"

Jocelyn nodded quickly. His Italian was good though accented. "That's right. I have a message for him from Hassan Saleem."

The boy frowned. "What do you know of Hassan?"

Jocelyn hesitated. She wasn't sure exactly who she was speaking to but he was very young, not more than eleven or twelve. To speak to him of murder when there might be no good reason seemed a senseless cruelty.

"I must talk with Jamal," she said.

"Why?" the boy demanded.

"Because Saleem sent me to him. I am looking for something."

The frown deepened. "For what?"

"I'm sorry but I can only discuss that with Jamal. Do you know him?"

"Perhaps." He came a few feet closer, still studying them cautiously. "Who are you?"

"My name is Jocelyn Merriman. I am the antiquities curator for a large auction house in New York. This is Professor Riordan Nolan. He is a scholar of antiquities."

At the mention of antiquities, the boy stiffened. He began to come closer still but then caught himself and stopped. "Jamal must be very careful."

"I understand that," Jocelyn said softly. "But surely Hassan would not have sent someone who could harm him."

"No," the boy agreed, "but who is to say you come from Hassan?"

"I have a letter from him."

The boy held out his hand. "Show it to me."

Jocelyn shook her head. "No, I will only show it to Jamal."

The boy fell silent. He looked at them both indecisively. For a moment, nothing moved. Then Riordan spoke gently in Arabic. At the first sound of his voice, the boy jumped slightly. But as Riordan went on, he seemed to grow in confidence.

"What are you saying to him?" Jocelyn asked.

"That sometimes it is necessary for a boy to be a man and that while caution is a good thing, it can also become an unwonted burden."

The boy seemed to agree for after a moment's further thought, he pedaled the bicycle over to the bench and got off. Joining them, he said simply, "I am Jamal."

Jocelyn had suspected as much, but she had hoped she

was wrong. As eager as she was to get on with the hunt, she didn't relish involving a child.

"How did you know Saleem?" she asked.

"He is my uncle." The boy hesitated. Apprehensively, he asked, "What news do you have of him?"

Jocelyn exchanged a quick glance with Riordan. There was nothing to do but tell him as gently as they could.

"I'm sorry," she said, "the news is not good. Saleem has died."

The boy absorbed this in silence. His features were delicate, the face dominated by large brown eyes, a straight bridged nose and a finely etched mouth. He was tall for his age and lean rather than muscular. His hair was neatly trimmed and his clothes simple but good. The more Jocelyn studied him, the more surprising he became.

All the more so because he did not shrink from the sadness she brought. "How did he die?" he asked.

Again, she looked at Riordan. He stepped in with simple honesty which in its own way was the greatest kindness he could offer.

"He was murdered in New York City. The authorities there are seeking the one who killed him. Before he died, he sent Miss Merriman a letter telling her to find you."

Jocelyn took the letter from her purse and handed it to Jamal. He scanned it quickly. "This is in English. I cannot read English."

That was a complication she had not expected although she should have. Quickly, she translated. "He said that he was concerned for his safety and worried that something might happen to him. If it did, I was to find Jamal at San Crisogono. He quoted a proverb from the fourth caliph and a teaching from the Koran."

Jamal smiled a shade tremulously. "That sounds like my uncle. He was a very learned man." He was silent for a time, struggling with his feelings, before he said, "I would not be alive today were it not for my Uncle Hassan. He brought me here from Beirut after the rest of my family was killed. He arranged for me to live with some people he knows—knew—and he came to see me whenever he could."

"When did you last see your uncle?" Riordan asked.

"Two weeks ago," Jamal said. His voice was thick. "He came suddenly in the night as he usually did. He couldn't stay but we spent a few hours together. He told me . . . he told me to work hard and do well in school and that I would have a good future."

"Did he tell you anything else?" Jocelyn asked. "Anything you might need to know in case something happened to him?"

Jamal shook his head. "No, he said nothing like that."

"Did he show you anything? Perhaps something very old with writing on it."

Again, the boy shook his head. "He showed me nothing."

"I don't understand," Jocelyn said. "Why did he send me to you if he didn't tell you or even show you anything?"

The boy did not reply. After a moment, Riordan said quietly, "Is it possible that you may have seen something your uncle didn't intend for you to see?"

Jamal shot him a startled look. "How did you know that?"

Riordan smiled. "It was a guess. My impression is that you had great respect and affection for your uncle. Naturally, you would not want to go against his wishes but perhaps something caught your eye. You may have seen it before you even realized that you weren't supposed to."

"I saw nothing old with writing on it," Jamal asserted.

"No," Riordan agreed. "I think what you saw was an ivory and gold cylinder."

Jocelyn was surprised but she kept silent, waiting for Jamal to confirm or deny this. Slowly, he said, "Yes, that is what I saw. It was in my uncle's bag. He had to take it somewhere. I wanted to go with him but he said it might be dangerous."

"But you loved your uncle," Riordan said, "did you not? And you would not want him in danger. When he left, you followed him?"

Slowly, Jamal nodded. "I did not mean to be disobedient but I was worried about him and also, I admit, I was curious. The cylinder was very beautiful."

"I think Saleem realized what you did," Jocelyn said. "Otherwise, he wouldn't have sent me here. And he could have sent you back. He must have decided that if you wanted so badly to see what he was doing, he would let you."

"But he didn't, lady. I followed him, yes, and maybe he did realize that for he was very clever about such things. But I never saw what he did with the cylinder."

At the look that passed between them, he added, "Truly, I did not. I fear you have come in vain."

"Not necessarily," Riordan said quickly. "There's still a chance that we might be able to find it. Can you show us where your uncle went?"

Jamal nodded. He stood up. "I will leave my bicycle with Mr. ben Ibraheim. The place is some distance from here."

Jocelyn and Riordan followed him back to the gaily

festooned stall where they were received by a grave Ahmed ben Ibraheim. He assured Jamal that the bicycle would be safe in his care.

They went then by bus and metro along a deliberately circuitous route. Saleem's inherent caution seemed to have been bred into the boy and Riordan approved. He had still not given up the idea that the encounter with the limousine was other than an accident.

Eventually, they stopped at a car rental office near one of the major hotels where Riordan secured a vehicle. The prospect of driving in Rome did not delight him but he accepted that there was no alternative.

Twilight was gathering by the time they reached their destination. It was a small house in the Castelli Romani district to the east of the city proper. The house was a two-story villa set amid pleasant gardens. It looked several centuries old but appeared to have been recently renovated.

"The house belongs to a friend of my uncle's," Jamal said. "But he is rarely in Rome. Hassan knew he was welcome to go there whenever he wished."

"But we aren't," Jocelyn said regretfully.

"That doesn't matter," Jamal said. "The night I followed him, my uncle didn't go into the house. He went around to the gardens in the back. I lost sight of him until he returned a short time later."

"It's hard to imagine where in a garden he would have thought it safe to leave the cylinder," Riordan said, "but it's all we've got."

Although the villa was clearly empty, they went cautiously into the garden. It was small, in keeping with the scale of the house itself, and was laid out in a series of triangular beds separated by gravel walks.

Toward the back of the garden, near the wall that separated the property from its neighbors, was a low mound of earth.

"If he buried it," Jocelyn said, "we'll never find it."

"Then he wouldn't have sent you," Riordan insisted, "or at least not without better instructions. What did that quote from the Koran say?"

" 'God guideth whom He will to His light.' Maybe, Saleem meant we'd find it if we were worthy, otherwise too bad."

"There was something more," Riordan said. "Something about a lamp."

"It's allegorical, a comparison of the light of God to the light of a sacred lamp." She looked around quickly. "I see what you're saying, but there aren't any lamps here."

"I know," Riordan admitted. "But there's got to be something."

"My uncle would not have brought us here without reason," Jamal insisted.

They wanted to agree but try though they did in the long minutes they searched the garden and the low mound, they could find nothing. At least not until Jocelyn stepped on a paving stone near the mound and felt the soft ground suddenly give way.

She struggled to keep her balance but without success. A hole opened beneath her and she fell, screaming, into darkness.

12

When Jocelyn disappeared, Riordan ran toward the last place he had seen her. There was nothing but a gaping hole in the ground. Soft dirt was still falling away into it. From below, he could hear her sobs, muffled but unmistakable.

Riordan didn't hesitate. He knew what he was about to do was foolish but he didn't question his reasons for doing it. His only thought was to get to Jocelyn in the quickest way possible. He stepped directly into the hole, fell straight down, and landed in a crouch. When he straightened, his head collided with the ground above.

He bent over slightly and shouted, "Jocelyn, where are you?"

"Here! Over here!" Her voice was weak and laced with fear. In the darkness, he could feel her frantic breathing and the pounding of her heart as he dragged her into his arms.

She was shaking so convulsively that he feared he wouldn't be able to hold her. Tightening his grip, he murmured, "It's all right. Everything's going to be okay. You didn't get hurt?"

She shook her head against his chest. "No, just terrified. Oh, God, Riordan—"

There was something undeniably satisfying about having a warm and beautiful woman clinging to him for comfort. Call it atavistic, call it primitive, call it what-the-hell, he was going to stop being a scientist and a scholar for at least a few minutes and enjoy being a man.

If enjoy was the right word. All that clinging had an implicit message—protect. He got it loud and clear, and he had no problem with it. The problem was protect from what?

Where were they? The dark was all-pervasive, he could see almost nothing. Only remnants of the twilight trickled down through the hole.

As his eyes adjusted, he had the sense of being in a fairly spacious chamber, low-ceilinged as he already knew, dry, and with the elusive aura of age he could never explain but recognized all the same.

"I'm not sure," he said, "but this could be the foundation of a building formerly on this site, or some sort of storage area, or maybe—"

He broke off as Jocelyn stiffened. A wavering beam of light had pierced the darkness. Slowly, it advanced toward them. As it grew closer, the shape behind it resolved into a smiling Jamal.

"Clever people," he said, his teeth shining whitely, "the friends of my uncle. When I saw what happened to you, I ran into the tool shed to find rope but instead I found the entrance to this place and this—" He gestured with the large flashlight only to freeze as the beam struck a recess in one of the walls.

Jamal stared at it for several moments before he realized what he was looking at. His bravado vanished. Quickly, he handed the flashlight to Riordan and stepped closer to both the adults.

"What is it?" Jocelyn asked. She stood up carefully. The ceiling was high enough for her to straighten fully. Only Riordan had to keep his head ducked.

"Catacombs," Riordan said. He shone the light in an arc off the surrounding walls. Numerous shelves or niches appeared to have been carved out of them. The light picked up small clusters of lumpy cloth covered with the dust of ages.

Jocelyn looked away hastily. She was not superstitious about such things, but invading the privacy of the dead inevitably gave her a queasy feeling. The light fell on a sightless skull gazing out from its timeless home. She took a quick step back and averted her eyes.

"I thought all the catacombs had been discovered," she said.

Riordan shook his head. He was looking around with unfeigned interest but then he would be, she thought tartly. To archaeologists, mass burial sites like this one were the equivalent of candy stores.

"The bigger ones were rediscovered in the sixteenth century," he said, "but it's always been known that there were smaller family cemeteries like this scattered around. Especially in the early years of the faith, Christians were dependent on the kindness of friends when it came to finding a place to bury their dead."

"There must have been an earlier villa here," Jocelyn said. She wrapped her arms around herself and tried not to shiver. "No wonder the ground is weak. They must have had to dig here extensively. Even worship services went on underground. Those were the days of the persecutions before Christianity was accepted as the official faith."

"A discovery like this would have prompted a visit from the antiquities commission," Riordan said, "and probably have delayed the renovations on the house. Rather than put up with that, they simply kept quiet."

Jamal, eyes wide, murmured, "But my uncle knew."

Jocelyn gave his hand a quick, reassuring squeeze. "I'm getting the impression your uncle knew a great many things. At any rate, it's a sensible enough place to hide an important artifact. We'd better start looking."

She sounded a good deal more eager than she felt. It was too much to ask that the cylinder would be out in plain sight. They would have to search for it, and the logical place to start were the niches. The thought of disturbing those huddled bundles of cloth and bone sent a chill through her.

All those niches—

She stopped, frozen in place, and stared straight ahead unseeingly. Niches. Niche. It wasn't a word that came up in everyday conversation yet she had encountered it recently enough. In the quote from the Koran Saleem had sent to her, the light of God had been described as a niche in which there was a lamp.

Riordan was moving toward the nearest burial shelf.

"Wait," she said, "Saleem sent us a clue." Briefly, she told him what she suspected. He nodded, agreeing that it was possible. Jamal's response more clearly mirrored her own, unfeigned relief.

"That must be it, lady," he said. "My uncle was a religious man but to choose those particular holy words, he must have had a reason. Let us leave the dead in peace and seek instead the lamp."

But search though they did from one end of the chamber to the other, they found nothing that resembled a lamp or a niche, much less a gold and ivory cylinder. After an hour, Riordan called a halt.

"We aren't getting anywhere. We'll have to search the bodies."

"Count me out," Jocelyn said. "I hate to be a wimp but I just can't see Saleem doing that. There has to be another explanation."

Riordan shook his head wearily. "I can't think of one."

He sat down beside her, holding the flashlight in his hands. The batteries were still going strong. They must have been fairly fresh. The single bulb flashed, starlike, in the darkness.

"Wait a minute . . ." Slowly, Riordan straightened. "What else did that quote say? The lamp encased in glass . . . From a blessed tree it is lighted . . . even though fire touched it not."

He laughed suddenly, the sound startling both Jocelyn and the boy.

"Jamal," he said, "was there another flashlight in the shed, one that didn't work?"

"Yes, but how did you—"

Riordan laughed again. "Your uncle was a devious old —never mind." He stood up and held out a hand to Jocelyn. "Come on."

"Where are we going?"

"To the shed. The way I see it, Saleem used the catacombs as a red herring. He must have figured anyone who got this far, but without specific instructions from him, would waste their time tearing through the old graves and go away empty-handed."

"How can you be so sure?" Jocelyn asked. They were climbing the worn stone steps that had formed the original entrance. Jamal was close behind them.

"I can't be," Riordan admitted. "But I've got a strong hunch."

They had reached the shed. It contained all the usual things found in such places. On a shelf set toward the back was the unworking flashlight. Riordan took hold of it carefully. It was made exactly like the one he had been using with a black plastic handle about twelve inches in length that was intended to hold a row of batteries.

Except in the case of the second flashlight, there were none. Riordan gently unscrewed the top and set it aside. He turned the casing with the opening pointed toward his palm. At first, Jocelyn saw nothing. Then her breath caught as the first glint of gold emerged.

"Oh, my—" she whispered. Jamal made a sound deep in his throat. Only Riordan appeared unmoved. Without attempting to remove the cylinder entirely, he screwed the top back on the flashlight. "Let's go," he said.

It was almost fully night by the time they left the shed and returned to the street in front of the villa. Their reemergence into the world left Jocelyn slightly dazed. The effort wasn't helped by Riordan's strange behavior. He shook his head, looking grim, and spread his hands, gesturing with the flashlight toward the back of the villa, and finally shrugged in apparent futility.

Jocelyn frowned. "What's that all about?"

Riordan continued to look disappointed and aggrieved but his voice was light. "Just in case anybody's watching, I'd like them to think we came away empty-handed." He continued pointing with the flashlight and shaking his head. Jamal fell in with him immediately. He hung his head as though in apology. Jocelyn made a halfhearted effort to go along but she wasn't feeling much up to play-acting.

All her thoughts were on the cylinder to the extent that she hardly noticed the car coming along the road in front of them. She saw it only out of the corner of her eye and it took several moments for it to register. Only then did she realize that the car was familiar, she had seen it before, near the trattoria in the Trastevere just as she had been setting out to find Ibraheim.

She touched Riordan's arm urgently. "We have to get out of here."

He shot her a quizzical look and followed her gaze to the car. His expression hardened. "Come on."

They jumped into the rental. Riordan was behind the wheel with Jocelyn in the passenger seat beside him. Jamal clambered into the back. The tires screeched as Riordan pressed the accelerator to the floor. Jocelyn was flung back against the seat. She clutched the flashlight he had tossed her and hung on for dear life.

At that hour, the quiet roads of the Castelli Romani were little used, unlike Rome itself where the streets would be bustling. Riordan took advantage of that to press the car to its limits. Following the twisting Via Tuscolana, they sped roughly southeast past meadows, olive groves, and vineyards dozing under the silver moon.

The road climbed through the Alban hills. Jocelyn caught a glimpse of water still as a mirror off in the distance but her attention was drawn by the large black car, still stubbornly pursuing them.

"We haven't lost them," she said.

Riordan nodded. "I know. Hang on."

Good advice but Jocelyn went further, she shut her eyes. Behind her, she heard Jamal inhale sharply and suspected he was doing the same.

Five minutes or so later, when she got up the nerve to open them again, the black car was no longer in sight. They were barreling along the Via Appia Nuova, in the general direction of Rome.

"What now?" Jocelyn asked. Croaked, actually. She cleared her throat and tried again.

Riordan grinned. He was enjoying himself. "Good question. Not back to the hotel, that's for sure. Jamal, who's likely to be worried if you don't turn up?"

"I stay with friends of my uncle. They will worry."

"We'll get word to them," Riordan said. "I don't think it's safe for you to go back there."

"Then where?" Jocelyn demanded.

Riordan thought for a moment. His choices were limited but that didn't matter. One was all he needed. "I'll come up with something," he said. "Meanwhile, get some rest. We've got a long drive."

For an hour and more, he kept watch in the rearview mirror in case the black car appeared again. When it did not, he relaxed slightly.

Jamal was asleep in the backseat. Jocelyn, despite her best efforts to stay awake, was dozing. She still held the flashlight on her lap. Riordan glanced at it, his eyes crinkling at the corners.

He was imagining his brother's reaction when Brendan realized the scroll was gone. He'd be none too pleased and neither, Riordan guessed, would be the men Brendan represented. It was just as well he was going to put a considerable number of miles between them and himself.

Off to his right, near the gleaming waters of Lake Albano, he could make out the high stone walls of Castle Gandalfo, the pope's summer residence. It was still too early in the year for the pontiff to be there but Riordan wondered all the same. There seemed to be an unusual number of lights burning as he sped past.

13

They caught the night ferry from Civitavecchia, the old port north of Rome. The journey to Sardinia took eight hours, and soon it would be a popular excursion for the throngs of tourists pouring into Italy. But right now the ferry was less than half full.

The boat was old but serviceable. Its decks smelled of decades of salt air and water mixing with the pungent aromas of sausage and garlic, old cheese and young wine carried on board in wicker baskets and eaten under the stars.

Paint peeled from the hull, and here and there patches of rust showed through. Cracked gray linoleum glowed yellow under the pale lights in metal cages that studded the ceiling of the main cabin. The lavatories were there and a small counter where drinks were sold but few people lingered. The night was pleasant and the camaraderie of a voyage, however brief, beckoned.

There were a few cabins below deck, mostly empty. Riordan secured one from the purser, an older man, burly and slightly disheveled, whose main function was discouraging disagreements among the passengers.

If questioned, he would remember Riordan, there was nothing to be done for that. But he did not see Jocelyn or Jamal who stayed on the car deck until Riordan returned for them.

"I may be being overly cautious," he said, "but I think it would be a good idea to stay out of sight as much as possible."

In fact, he did not think he was being too cautious at all. He said that only to prevent them from worrying too much. So far, everything had gone extremely well. He did not make the mistake of thinking that would necessarily continue.

Brendan was very much on his mind, although he would not say so.

While Riordan laid out the food they had brought for a simple supper, Jocelyn used the ladies room to freshen up. She splashed cold water on her face, gave her hair a quick brush, and wished she'd had the foresight to pack a toothbrush. She supposed her belongings would be safe enough at the hotel. The room was booked for a week and if she wasn't back by then her luggage would be put in storage; Riordan's as well.

She returned to the cabin and they settled down to eat. Jamal remained subdued and silent, but of the three he was the only one who did justice to the meal. Youth, Jocelyn thought, and gave him a smile.

"We owe you our thanks," she said.

He nodded but his mood remained somber. "I did as my uncle wished, but that does not change anything, does it? He is still dead."

Jocelyn's throat tightened. The boy had been so brave that it was easy to forget he was still a child. She reached out a hand and covered his.

"Nothing can change that," she said gently, "but at least now that we have the cylinder we're that much closer to finding out why Hassan was killed."

"And by whom," Riordan added. He met Jamal's eyes across the narrow expanse of the cabin. Jocelyn saw the look that passed between them, a purely male look of realities accepted and pledges made.

A short time later, Riordan suggested that they try to get some sleep. Jamal took the top bunk with Riordan in the one under him and Jocelyn on the other side of the cabin. The boy fell asleep almost immediately. Youth again, Riordan thought, and resisted any further thoughts about how it was wasted on the young.

He turned on his side so that he could see Jocelyn. She lay facing him with the rough brown blanket pulled up over her. Her eyes met his briefly but he could read nothing through the thick fringe of her lashes. After a moment, they closed. He did not presume that she slept, only that she preferred to be alone with her thoughts.

Between them, on the floor propped up against Riordan's bunk, lay the rucksack he had bought on the way to the ferry. The flashlight was in it along with a selection of maps, a bottle of sun lotion, several granola bars, and assorted other items travelers could legitimately be carrying.

Inside the flashlight was the cylinder. There had been no time to examine it since leaving Rome and Riordan felt no temptation to do so now. He could wait, containing the urgency within him, until the circumstances were right.

He looked at Jocelyn again. Her breathing had slowed, become more regular. Above him, he could hear Jamal murmur softly to himself in a dream. A memory, unbidden, returned to him of other nights, listening to his men sleeping, and feeling the burden of his responsibility for keeping them safe in a situation where he knew he could not.

It was the same now, yet different. This time, he knew the enemy far better, could indeed see his face. The face of his brother. That it was also his own face did not trouble him.

For all his scholarly bent, he was not an unduly pensive man. He was who he was; Brendan was who he was. That they stood on opposite sides did not surprise him; it had happened often enough before. But never with the stakes so high.

He found himself almost hoping that clever, dead Saleem had been tricked or trickster, either one would do. That whatever lay within the gold and ivory cylinder was of no particular consequence instead of what he suspected it to be. He would know soon enough and then—

The rest would wait. He closed his eyes and let the gentle rocking of the ferry take him.

Mist rose from the water but the sky above was already crystalline blue. Between the two, as though adrift in a world of its own making, lay Sardinia. The island was mountainous, covered with low scrub bushes, sparsely populated. Jocelyn could make out bright, whitewashed houses, smoke curling from their chimneys, and dark winding ribbons of road leading away into the looming hills.

She heard a sound behind her and turned away from the porthole. Riordan was awake. He sat up, running a hand through his tumbled hair. A night's growth of beard shadowed the hard line of his jaw. His eyes swept over her, missing nothing.

She swallowed against the tightness in her throat and managed a smile. "It looks like a different world," she said, gesturing in the direction she had been looking. She spoke softly; Jamal still slept with the easy unconsciousness of his years, and she didn't want to disturb him before it was necessary.

"It is, in some ways," Riordan said, also pitching his voice low. He came and stood beside her at the porthole, glancing out into the bright morning. "The Romans never really managed to put their stamp on the place and neither did anyone who came later. Geography and sheer luck combined to keep it off the beaten track."

"Yet you have a friend here," she reminded him, "about whom you've said very little. What makes you think he'll be so anxious to take us in?"

Riordan smiled slightly. "Let's just say he likes a mystery, and he isn't a stranger to risks."

"Sounds fascinating. Are you sure he can be trusted?"

"Implicitly." Again, the smile appeared. "He's of the old school. The sort of man you'd be lucky to have at your back when things get tough."

"Do you expect them to?" she asked.

His eyes slid away from her. He put his hands in his pockets and shrugged. "Don't worry about it."

Which told her more than she really wanted to know.

The house was in the hills above Cagliari, far enough away from the bustling harbor town for serenity's sake but close enough for convenience. It stood surrounded by gnarled olive trees older than the building itself, or indeed than memory, and by fragrant junipers whose scent carried on the constant wind.

Whitewashed walls dotted with green shuttered windows were topped by a red-tiled roof that was barely visible from the largely untraveled road. Visitors who happened to wander by could easily miss it.

That suited the house's master for he was a man who valued his privacy almost as much as he valued the simple fact of life itself. His name was Sir David Hargreave and he had been, until recently, head of British MI5.

His retirement was precipitated by the explosion of a blood vessel deep within his brain. In the aftermath of that, lying in the hospital bed with an assortment of tubes and wires protruding from him, he had discovered that he truly wanted to live.

That had surprised him somewhat for there was no possibility of his returning to the work that had been the structure and substance of his existence. Yet life held other opportunities.

He had his wife, Penelope, whom he truly loved and who had always been his link to what he thought of as the daylight world, the one he fought from the shadows to protect. And he had his hobby, some said his passion, although that wasn't fair to Penelope.

He would reject the claim, but in fact he was a better than average amateur archaeologist with a discerning eye and a mind sensitive to the whispers of departed glory trapped within fragments of the past, much as the deep, eternal rumbling of the ocean was caught within the hidden chambers of an abandoned shell.

His friendship with Riordan Nolan was as unlikely as it was steadfast. They had met three years before when Riordan was digging in Greece and Sir David was part of a group of enthusiasts who signed on to help.

The two men fell to talking around the fire late at night when the others, exhausted by the heat and labor, were asleep. They spoke of many things and left a great deal more unsaid. Between them grew an awareness of shared perceptions—that the world was a dangerous place, that there were things worth fighting for, that they had each peered into the abyss sufficiently to confront their own worst fears and be the better for it.

They became friends. Enough so that when he heard Riordan's voice on the other end of the phone, Sir David knew at once the cause for the strange sense of waiting that had lately settled over him and also that it was over.

He dropped a last spadeful of manure on a specimen of tea rose in the hope that it would feel suitably encouraged. Pen persisted in trying to grow roses despite a climate that didn't really suit them, and he did what he could to help. But he much preferred the native delphiniums and adonis, the so-called pheasant's eye, that flourished on their own.

Straightening, he removed his battered Panama and touched a handkerchief to his brow. He was standing thus, looking out toward the road, when the dusty car heaved its way around the last winding turn and slid to a stop near him.

Riordan stepped from behind the wheel. He looked tired but resolute. From the passenger side, a tall, attractive woman exited. A young boy got out of the back and stood, gazing around, like a wary fawn.

Sir David put the shovel down and went to greet them.
He spared only a passing glance for the knapsack Riordan
carried, the strap looped twice around his wrist. There
would be time for that later.

14

By mid-morning, the tourists had fled the simmering heat of the Piazza di San Pietro, seeking shelter in the cool, shadowed depths of the basilica or elsewhere amid the Vatican grounds. Only a solitary figure moved across the broad paving stones, head down, working diligently with pole and pick to remove the few scraps of litter blown about by the dry wind.

Brendan Nolan watched the figure for a few moments before turning away from the high windows. Behind him, in the marbled stillness of the cardinal's office, a throat was cleared.

The sound came from Monsignor Giovanni Ricci, in his mid-forties, slender and long-boned with dark hair cropped close to his skull, darker eyes, and pale, unmarred skin. In this palace of popes, where self-denial was regarded as an aberration, Ricci seemed a throwback to an earlier, simpler era. Not that anyone found that laudable.

In the polished corridors, behind the gilded mirrors,

around the darker corners, memories lingered of the centuries when terror was the handmaiden of holiness. They were an embarrassment now, those times of brand and fire, rack and wheel, shoved far back in the closet of the mind where the howling could be only dimly heard.

For all that, men such as the Monsignor still had their uses, never more than in these days of struggle to bring new order to Holy Mother Church. Brendan reminded himself of that as he repressed the instinctive spurt of dislike he always felt when confronted by Ricci.

Cooly, he said, "The cardinal is well?"

Ricci nodded once, a short jab of the head that revealed little. "He would be better if you had done your job. Your confidence in your brother was misplaced."

Brendan shrugged, seemingly unperturbed. "Was it? We had no idea where the scroll was hidden or even how to take the first steps toward finding it. Now that problem is solved. We are no longer looking for a small, easily concealed object. We are looking for a man, one whose behavior is not entirely unpredictable."

A corner of Ricci's mouth lifted scornfully. "Indeed, he can be expected to do whatever is unfavorable to the church. Or had you forgotten that he is a heretic?"

Brendan's eyes narrowed. He was willing to tolerate much from Ricci only because he refused to take the man seriously. But the use of that word with all the ominous weight it carried made him think twice about his strategy.

He looked away again, squinting at the relentless white glare bouncing off the exterior palace walls. His voice was muted in the stillness. "Don't be ridiculous."

"How American of you," Ricci said. He was smiling again. His teeth were slightly yellowed, making him look wolfish.

"Everything is questionable, everything can be doubted, isn't that how you see it? But in fact there is no room for doubt. The church is not and never will be a democracy."

"Spare me the lecture," Brendan said wearily. He had heard it all too often, the same tired old clichés trotted out as justification for stifling dissent. That was the real trouble with men like Ricci, there was never anything original about them.

"I will find Riordan," he said. "There are a limited number of places he can be. He will listen to reason."

Ricci folded his hands against his cassock, the fingers curling around each other. "I shall pray that is true, but remember the sin of pride can strike us all, particularly when we least expect it. This is not a private mission, Father Nolan, make no mistake about that. You are responsible to others."

"I will be happy to discuss this matter with the cardinal at any time—"

"The cardinal has turned the matter over to me," Ricci said. His satisfaction was unmistakable. He had been saving this, waiting for precisely the right moment, and he had found it.

Brendan paled slightly. "That is—surprising."

"Indeed? Why? Because you think I am a poor choice for such a task? But that is your pride again, Father Nolan, that leads you to believe men like you are superior to men like me. You should work to temper such failings of character."

He paused, observing the effect of his words. All things considered, it was less than satisfactory. Brendan refused to be baited. He waited, silent, his eyes never leaving Ricci's face until the other man was forced to glance away.

"You will report to me daily," Ricci said, his lips tight, "as to your progress or lack thereof. Is that understood?"

"Perfectly." Brendan squared his shoulders. He glanced at the pedestal clock on the mantel. "Since the cardinal is unavailable, I should be getting back to work." He started toward the door, seemed to think better of it, and turned around again. "Presuming you have no objection?"

A pulse beat in Ricci's jaw. "You have one week. If the scroll has not been recovered by then, other measures will be taken."

Brendan's mouth tightened. There was a great deal he could have said—about arrogance, stupidity, and the deadly harm both were doing to his beloved church. But it would have been a waste of breath.

He walked away in silence, down the long corridor bathed in sunlight, past the various Vatican offices where the business of the church went on, day in and day out, year after year, century after century, a vast bureaucracy grinding away for the greater glory of God.

The corridor was hushed and only distant sounds reached him from behind the office doors. Yet he could hear the howling, louder now. A shadow moved across the sun, plunging the marbled corridor into momentary darkness.

Deep in his bones, he felt a chill. There was much to do and very little time left in which to do it. He had told Ricci he could find Riordan but in truth, he had no such confidence.

His brother had the scroll; it was only a matter of time before he realized its full significance. And when he did—

At the end of the corridor was a flight of steps. Brendan took them two at a time. He entered his own office and went directly to his desk. His secretary was at lunch. He would have an interval to himself. His hand hesitated over the phone. It occurred to him suddenly that the phone could be tapped.

He went out again, down the stairs, and out into the sun-drenched piazza. Crossing it quickly, he exited onto a narrow side street. From there, he walked until he found a small osteria that he remembered had a public phone in the back. In the cool, wine-scented shadows, he made his call.

"A nice piece of work," Sir David said. He turned the cylinder over in his hands. An air of suppressed excitement hung over him, evidenced in the gleam of his eyes and the flush of color high on his cheeks. His hands, touching the finely wrought turtledoves that formed the end caps, were surpassingly gentle.

"A bit out of my area. What would you say—eighth, ninth century?"

"More likely ninth," Jocelyn said. She instinctively liked this big, gentle-faced man but she sensed there was more to him than might be expected in a retired British civil servant.

For one thing, there was the matter-of-fact way he had received Riordan's explanation of why they were there and what they had with them. The sudden appearance of an ancient artifact that already had at least one murder associated with it did not faze Sir David at all.

As Riordan had said, he was a man accustomed to dealing with risks.

"The workmanship is Byzantine," she said, "which isn't surprising. Even after the Moslems took over Palestine in the seventh century, they continued to trade with Constantinople."

"Then the Khalduns would have had ready access to such an object," Sir David said.

Riordan nodded. He had outlined what they knew so far, including the contents of the diary left by Lorenzo di Costello. As he did so, he watched their reactions, Jamal's in particular.

Riordan thought, although he couldn't be sure, that the boy was hiding something. There was a quick veiling of his eyes to conceal what?—surprise, awareness? It was impossible to tell.

They were all standing around the worn pine table in the library. It was a big, airy room that looked out over the garden. Three of the four walls were covered with floor-to-ceiling bookshelves, some of them bowing in the middle from the weight they carried.

A quick glance was enough to confirm that the Hargreaves' interests were eclectic, covering everything from *Advances in Hybridization of Roses* to *The Euro-Asian Federation in the 21st Century—an Economic Primer.*

Which was not to say that the lighter side was neglected. Sir David appeared to be a fan of the shoot-'em-up variety of international thriller, while Lady Penelope seemed to favor cozy relationship novels with a soupçon of glitz and glitter.

She was a tall, slender woman in her sixties, very attractive still with silvered blond hair and the perfect rose-petal complexion of a Sargent portrait. Her gaze as it fell on her husband was tender, a bit indulgent, but with an undercurrent of worry Jocelyn wondered at.

"There is no inscription," Riordan said, "but there are traces of wax along the top as well as the fragments of a seal. The break looks fairly recent since the edges of the seal are still sharp."

"Saleem opened the cylinder," Jocelyn said. "He would have had to in order to photocopy the section of the scroll he showed me."

Riordan nodded. "But until then, it looks as though whatever was in here was kept locked away."

"Locked away where?" Jocelyn murmured, almost to herself. There were so many questions to be answered, so many possibilities. They had barely begun to scratch the surface of the mystery presented by the Magdalen Scroll, if indeed that was what lay within the cylinder. If they—

She broke off, staring at Riordan. His gaze flicked around the table, studying them each in turn but lingering a moment on her. As she watched, he seemed to come to some decision.

"Who knows?" he said.

"What about the turtledoves?" Sir David asked. "Any ideas about their significance?"

"Only the obvious," Jocelyn replied. "They're a standard emblem for peace, love, rebirth, that sort of thing. I imagine the Khalduns had the cylinder made and probably chose the design to reflect what was on the scroll inside."

She looked to Riordan for confirmation of that but he merely shrugged. "Enough speculating. Let's see what we've got."

They all leaned forward slightly as Riordan twisted the top of the cylinder off and laid it carefully aside. He peered into the interior.

"It's a scroll, all right, evenly wound but with no space between the material and the inside of the cylinder." He looked at Sir David. "I could use a pair of tweezers."

The Englishman nodded. He got up and returned a moment later. Working with great care, Riordan applied the tweezers to the innermost curl of the scroll. By fractions of an inch, he tightened the material just enough to release it from the cylinder. It slid into his hand and was laid gently on the table.

Jocelyn stared at it. The scroll was about eight inches long and three inches in diameter, bulkier than Jocelyn had expected. It had a dry, slightly yellow appearance and the exposed end was frayed. Belatedly aware that she had been holding her breath, she let it go and said, "Now what?"

"Now the work begins," Riordan said. "Sir David, if I might have your assistance?"

Together, the two men slowly and painstakingly unrolled the scroll. No one else moved as they did so. Jocelyn's hands were painfully clenched. If the scroll was too delicate, if Saleem's handling of it had damaged it in any way, if luck simply wasn't with them . . .

But so far as she could see, the scroll was intact and the unrolling did not harm it. Fully opened, it stretched three feet in length and was covered with tightly written columns of script written in a brown ink interspersed with a few rusty stains.

"Aramaic," Sir David said, bending over for a closer look.

Riordan nodded. "First century Christian Era, if the fragment is anything to go by. The vocabulary indicates Palestinian origin."

The two men exchanged a look. "Consistent, at least," Sir David murmured.

Riordan shrugged. "We'll see. Will I find the necessary reference texts here?"

"I think so. If there is anything else you need, I can acquire it fairly easily. There are a number of enthusiastic amateurs on the island."

"I'd prefer to keep this very quiet," Riordan said, his eyes still on the scroll. He reached out a finger, not quite touching it as he traced a line of script.

Sir David nodded. "Of course." He hesitated a moment, watching his young friend. "I really do think you'll find everything you need."

Riordan didn't appear to hear him. He was already lost in the tantalizing puzzle the scroll presented.

Sir David touched his wife's arm lightly. He nodded to Jocelyn and Jamal. "I suggest we leave him to it. The rest of us will only be in the way."

Lady Penelope led them out. Jamal went readily but Jocelyn lingered a moment. Riordan was bending over the table, his brow furrowed. He seemed to be hesitating.

"Good luck," she murmured, unsure that he heard her and wondering what she was really wishing for him. The scroll had killed Saleem and—if di Costello was to be believed—almost the entire Khaldun family. How many other deaths had it caused over the centuries?

Holiest among holy, di Costello had said, without offering any explanation for what he meant. Surely that did not apply to the writings of Mary Magdalen, no matter how interesting, significant, or provocative they might be. Something else was involved here, something Jocelyn could not begin to fathom. But Riordan was about to try.

The sudden, inexplicable urge to protect him left her shaken. It was as irrational a desire as she had ever felt in her life yet she could not shake it. Not even after she went back out into the bright sunlight and the heedless day.

15

"I think you'll be comfortable here," Lady Penelope said, "but if there's anything else you need, just let me know."

Jocelyn looked around the small, whitewashed cottage that stood a few dozen yards away from the main house and shook her head bemusedly. "I can't imagine what else I could possibly need. This is lovely."

She wasn't exaggerating. The cottage was furnished with wooden tables and cabinets painted in soft pastels, handwoven rugs, couches and chairs heaped with pillows, bright pottery, and—incongruously but delightfully—American quilts in a riot of colors.

There were two bedrooms in addition to the combined living area and kitchen, and a bath that had a wall of glass looking out across windswept vistas uninterrupted by so much as a road.

"I'll put Professor Nolan in here as well," Lady Penelope said, "if that's all right with you. Jamal will be in the main house."

Jocelyn smiled slightly. Her hostess was a model of discretion. The two bedrooms removed any presumption that she and Riordan were intimate with each other while the cottage's privacy left the matter entirely in their own hands.

"That's fine," she said. "Thank you for the loan of the clothes. I'm afraid we left in a hurry."

"It's no trouble at all," Lady Penelope replied. "When you've settled in, why don't you come out to the pool? We can have a nice chat."

The way she said it, her hostess might have intended nothing more than a talk about the weather but Jocelyn doubted it. Left to her own devices, she took a quick shower, luxuriating in washing the grime of the ferry from her, and put on the swimsuit that was among the items Lady Penelope had provided.

Also included were half a dozen cotton slacks and tops, sun cream and moisturizer, a robe and several night-gowns, and even a toothbrush. Sir David's wife seemed to have a good deal of experience dealing with unexpected guests, including those who dropped in without any of the usual accoutrements. Jocelyn could only wonder where she had acquired it.

She left the cottage and walked along the flower-bordered path to the back of the house. Lady Penelope saw her and raised a hand in greeting. She was stretched out on a chaise longue beside the pool, wearing a swimsuit that looked similar to the one Jocelyn had on, with her silver-blond hair tucked up under a battered straw hat, and an unread book lying unattended beside her.

"He swims very well," she said as Jocelyn sat down beside her. Indeed, Jamal was cutting a brown swath through the water. He came up for air, saw them, and grinned. For the first time since Jocelyn had met him, he looked like an ordinary thirteen-year-old boy unburdened by grief or worry.

"He's a good kid," she said softly. "I know plenty of adults who couldn't have handled this business as well."

"Hassan Saleem was his guardian?"

Jocelyn nodded. "And his uncle. Jamal's been living with some people in Rome but they aren't actually relatives. He called them before we came here and said he would be away for a while. They didn't object."

"Is it possible they were relieved?" Lady Penelope asked softly. She glanced again at the boy frolicking in the pool.

"I suppose. With Hassan dead money would be an issue, and they may also fear that whatever struck him down could somehow be a threat to them."

"They might not be wrong," Lady Penelope said. "This is all very strange. A testament by Mary Magdalen? Why has no one heard of it before?"

"There have always been rumors, but they were discounted because there was no real evidence that such a testament existed. However, there have been other writings from the early Christian era that claimed a much greater role for Mary Magdalen than the church fathers accorded her."

"I'd certainly like to think that was true," Lady Penelope said. "But it doesn't explain why there would be so much fuss."

"It concerns the question of whether or not women should be priests. The justification for barring us from the priesthood rests on the assertion that all the disciples of Christ were male and therefore all priests should be too."

"I can never follow that kind of reasoning," Lady Penelope said. "The idea that what has been must always be seems the height of folly to me. But never mind. Couldn't the Vatican simply say that whatever is in the scroll isn't necessarily true and they're not going to be influenced by it, so there?"

"I suppose," Jocelyn said. "That may be exactly the position they take once they find out about all this."

The sun was very bright. She shaded her eyes from it and watched as Jamal climbed onto the diving board. "He's said very little about his uncle but I have the impression he has nowhere to go. At least, he hasn't mentioned any possibility."

"I'm not surprised," Lady Penelope said. "He's Lebanese. With all the turmoil in that part of the world, there are far too many homeless children." She was silent again, watching, before she said, "He seems like a bright boy."

"He is," Jocelyn agreed. "And he has courage. When Riordan and I disappeared into the catacombs, he didn't panic but simply set about finding us. I wish there was something I could do for him."

"Don't worry about it," Lady Penelope said. She settled back on the chaise longue and closed her eyes. "David's on the phone right now. He'll work it out."

Jocelyn shot her a surprised look which her hostess did not see. She wanted to ask what Sir David could do for Jamal, especially by merely working the phone, but it seemed rude to do so. Instead, she had to content herself with her own speculation which proved entertaining enough.

"Was Sir David in the foreign service?" Jocelyn asked.

Lady Penelope did not open her eyes but she did give a little shake of her head. "That's what people have always been told but he was with MI5 for thirty years including several years as chief before he retired."

She opened one eye a slit and laughed at Jocelyn's expression. "Don't look so surprised. It's rather like your CIA, people always know who's the head of that, don't they? We're all very open about this sort of thing now. I have to admit I rather miss the days when I could say my husband was in tariff administration and bring a grinding halt to any conversation."

"How do you happen to know Riordan?" Jocelyn asked, wondering where the paths of an ancient historian and the former head of one of the world's top security agencies had crossed.

"After David retired, we went to Greece on a dig. It had always been something of a dream deferred for him. Beastly hard work, if you ask me, but he got a tremendous kick out of it. Did him a world of good. Riordan was in charge. They hit it off immediately, spent all their time after hours cloistered together talking about this lovely bit of pottery and that particularly nice scrap of papyrus. At least I think that's what they talked about, it's difficult to know with men like them."

Jocelyn was tempted to ask what sort of men Lady Penelope thought they were, and why she lumped together the former head of one of the world's top security agencies with a teacher and scholar, but just then Sir David came to join them.

He nodded to Jocelyn as he sat down on the edge of his wife's chair. Her hand slipped into his with the ease of a gesture much repeated over the years, becoming so familiar that only its omission would have been noticed.

"So?" Lady Penelope asked.

Sir David shrugged and allowed himself a small smile.

"I'll speak with the boy very soon. I think he'll be pleased."

Lady Penelope nodded. "The Jensens?"

"You agree, don't you?"

"Oh, yes. Life in Surrey will do him a world of good. He can go to MacLean and then who knows? Eton certainly isn't out of the question, as bright as he seems."

"Excuse me," Jocelyn said. It seemed right to apologize for intruding, for though neither of the Hargreaves would ever dream of giving such an impression or even think it, the intimacy between them was so palpable and rare as to demand acknowledgment, at least so far as Jocelyn was concerned.

"It's wonderful that you're willing to help Jamal," she went on, "but Surrey is in England, isn't it? Aren't there legal restrictions on a child his age entering the country?"

"That really isn't a problem," Sir David said. He offered no further explanation, apparently considering that none was needed.

Sometime later, after Jamal had finally tired of the pool, Sir David took him off for a stroll around the gardens. When they returned, the young boy looked as though he had been made the possessor of a great and utterly unexpected gift. His attitude was one of grave elation.

"Have you heard?" he asked Jocelyn. "I am going to England."

"That's wonderful," she said, truly glad for him if still a bit dazzled by the speed with which it had all been arranged.

"I am to live with the family of Mr. Thomas Jensen, who is a teacher at a very good school for boys. He will prepare me to start there next year."

"Tom spent several years in Lebanon," Sir David explained. "He speaks Arabic as well as a slew of other languages. He's a good fellow, married to a friend of Pen's. They've got two boys and have no qualms about adding another."

"I'm sure you will do very well," Jocelyn told Jamal, and meant it.

She lingered a while longer at the pool, swimming a little until the effort and her own preoccupations drove her back to the chaise. Lying there, her eyes closed, she reviewed the events of the last few days and tried to define what was troubling her. It was all going so well and yet she couldn't shake the niggling feeling that something was wrong, or out of place, or simply as yet unexplained.

She gave up finally and went back to the quiet cottage where she showered again to wash the sun lotion off her skin, and dressed in a set of the simple cottons Lady Penelope had given her. She had seen nothing of Riordan since leaving him in the library. It was getting on for dinner and he still had not reappeared. A quick peek in the cottage's second bedroom confirmed that the clothes and toiletries left for him had not been touched.

The light outside was fading to a soft purple blue when Jocelyn walked down the path toward the main house. Lanterns cast soft illumination across the stone patio. Sir David had changed into gray slacks, a sports shirt, and a blue blazer. He stood beside a trolley mixing drinks. Lady Penelope was nearby, wearing an ankle-length cotton dress in a bright Liberty print. She smiled when she saw Jocelyn.

"There you are. Feeling better?"

"Tremendously. Have you seen Riordan?"

"Still in the library," Sir David answered. "I looked in on him a while ago."

Jocelyn accepted a Campari and soda. She asked, "Any idea how it's going?"

"Not well by the look of it. He seems bogged down but don't be concerned about that. These things always seem to go that way."

Lady Penelope excused herself to check on dinner. She assured Jocelyn she could manage. "I've kept it simple. We generally have a couple looking after us but when Riordan called, we thought it might be better if they had some time off." She disappeared into the house.

"Jamal will be joining us shortly," Sir David said. "I've given him a book about English social customs written by a fascinating Arab gentleman, Muhammad al-Kasim, who traveled there in the late nineteenth century. At the time, we Britishers were turning out volumes by the thousands about our adventures in various exotic locales, including Kashmir where Mr. al Kasim happened to come from. It seems only fair that someone turned the tables on us."

He took another sip of his drink and added, "The really interesting thing about the book is how little in it has changed, at least so far as places like Surrey and Mac-Lean's are concerned."

Jocelyn smiled at the thought of Jamal being prepared for his new life by reading the travel recollections of an Arab gentleman of the previous century. "I'm still amazed at how quickly you've arranged everything."

Sir David shrugged modestly. "At the risk of sounding cynical, knowing the right people can accomplish wonders." He paused for a moment, looking at her. "But I imagine you know that, Miss Merriman. Holcroft & Farnsworth is itself hardly without influence."

"That's true," she agreed. "Did Riordan tell you I worked for them?"

"As a matter of fact, he didn't. I recalled seeing you at an auction about a year ago. Greco-Roman bronzes."

Jocelyn remembered the auction, it had gone very well. But she didn't recall seeing Sir David. "I'm sorry—"

"No reason you should be. There was a great deal going on and I only bid for one piece, which I am happy to say I got."

"Good for you. Do you buy often?"

"Not since prices went through the roof. The run up on antiquities has been astounding. No, I was lucky enough to put a few things together years ago when you could still do that and not end up hog-tied to the bankers."

"Riordan has some definite opinions on that subject. He thinks antiquities shouldn't be sold at all."

"A case can be made for that, but I rather think he takes the extreme position simply to provoke debate. He likes that kind of thing, you know."

"You mean argument?" Jocelyn asked dryly. "The clash of minds, sound and fury?"

Sir David laughed. "He's a good man for a dustup."

"Funny, he said almost the same thing about you. That you're the kind of man he'd want at his back."

Her host looked pleased. "Did he really? How extraordinary. Have you known him long?"

"We met when I was a student at Columbia and he was teaching there. But our acquaintance was brief and we didn't see each other again until just a short time ago. Of course," she added, "I was aware of his work."

"Yes, you'd have to be, being in the business. Tell me, where does Holcroft & Farnsworth stand on the matter of the Magdalen Scroll?"

"Obviously, we would like to be agents for its sale, but," she added quickly, "authenticity and provenance have to be clearly established before we could do anything."

"Saleem's death complicates that a great deal. How much do you know about him?"

"Almost nothing," Jocelyn admitted. "I only met him once. He offered no explanation for how he had come into possession of the scroll. Obviously, had he lived I would have pressed him on that."

"You realize there is a possibility it was stolen?"

"Of course."

"That doesn't disturb you?"

"Not automatically. The question then becomes whether the person it was stolen from had a legal right to it in the first place. What we try to do is track an object back to its last point of legal ownership and deal with that person, presuming he or she still exists. Failing that, we try to locate the heirs. It can get very complicated and some cases take years to straighten out, but the mere fact that an object may have been stolen, even numerous times, doesn't mean it can never be legally sold."

"I see," Sir David said. He stared off into the gathering night for a moment before going on. "I made certain inquiries about Mr. Saleem. He was a rather shadowy figure involved in moving large sums of money for people who like to be discreet about such things. He operated under various aliases of which Hassan Saleem was merely one. I have no idea of his real name. At any rate, the kind of world he lived in would have afforded him numerous opportunities for skulduggery but there's no indication that he took advantage of them. All things considered, he comes across quite well."

"I won't ask how you know all this," Jocelyn said quietly, "but I gather it had an impact on your willingness to help Jamal?"

"I would have done that anyway, but I admit knowing the character of the uncle makes it easier to recommend the nephew. The point is that Saleem wouldn't have been an obvious choice to act as middleman in a situation like this. Offhand, I can think of a dozen people who would have been logical candidates, and there are undoubtedly many more, but he wasn't one of them."

"Then perhaps it wasn't stolen," Jocelyn suggested. "It may have been sold by someone who didn't recognize its value."

"Perhaps."

Sir David said little more and a short time later Lady Penelope called them in to dinner. It was a pleasant meal of lamb and rice well seasoned by Jamal's enthusiastic recounting of all he had learned so far. Jocelyn enjoyed it. But afterward, when she had said her good nights and returned to the cottage, she couldn't shake the sense that her conversation with Sir David had not been entirely by chance.

He had wanted to say certain things to her—or ask certain questions—and had arranged an opportunity for them to be alone for that purpose. It would have been easy enough to do that with Riordan somewhere off in the first century, Jamal totally absorbed in England, and Lady Penelope long schooled to such matters. But why bother?

His interest seemed focused on the provenance of the scroll; had it been stolen or not? He went out of his way to describe Hassan Saleem as a man unlikely to traffic in illegal artifacts.

But then how had it come into his possession and, even more to the point, where had the scroll lain in the years since di Costello claimed it had been taken under guard to Rome? Almost a thousand years needed to be accounted for.

Her head swam at the thought. She glanced toward the house, noticing the light still on in the library. Presumably, at some point Riordan would remember that he needed food and rest but it was impossible to say when.

The thought that she'd missed something was back in full force, distracting her. She went out into the cottage's small kitchen and made herself a cup of herbal tea. Sipping it, she paced across the living area, looking out into the darkness, struggling to think.

And then she remembered. In all the tumult of the last few days, and perhaps also because of her own unruly feelings, she had refused to confront what was staring her right in the face. She had let at least one piece of information and possibly more go by without following up as she should have.

Jocelyn Merriman was not the sort of woman to make a scene, but Josie Mulkowsky felt no such restraint. She covered the path to the house in record time and walked into the library just as Riordan was about to call it a night.

16

"**H**ow did you know about the cylinder?"

Riordan looked up from the table where he had been working and squinted slightly. He was tired, his shoulders and neck hurt, and he had just realized that he was very hungry.

A glance out the window showed that it was night which surprised him. When he had last thought to notice, the sun had been shining.

He sighed, rubbed a hand over his eyes and said, "About time."

Jocelyn bristled. It was bad enough that she'd let it slip; if he was going to rub her nose in it, there'd be hell to pay. "I've been busy," she said. "Now give, how did you know?"

Riordan sat back in his chair and looked at her. It was a thoroughly comprehensive look that went from the top of her head to her toes. It left her flushed.

"How about I read it in di Costello?"

"No dice. He never mentioned the cylinder. It was remembering that that finally made me realize what I'd missed. When we first met Jamal and were trying to figure out what he knew, you asked if he'd seen an ivory and gold cylinder in his uncle's possession. How did you know?"

He hesitated just long enough to make her think he wasn't going to answer. Finally, he said, "My brother told me."

Jocelyn stared at him. "Your brother. What brother?"

"I have a brother. His name is Brendan Nolan and he's a Catholic priest."

A melange of images flashed through Jocelyn's mind— Riordan standing up in front of a class talking about the power and beauty of an ancient culture; Riordan declaiming on the endless need to question, doubt, challenge everything and anything; Riordan being funny and tender; Riordan seductive and passionate; Riordan—

"You're kidding?"

"Not only that, he's my twin."

"You're telling me there is someone who looks just like you running around loose and that he's a Catholic priest?"

Riordan nodded. "Not just like, we're fraternal twins. In some ways, we're about as different as anyone could imagine. Brendan works at the Vatican."

Jocelyn prided herself on never being one to jump to conclusions, but she was getting a very bad feeling. A priest at the Vatican. Unless she missed by a mile, guess who was lining up to claim ownership of the scroll?

"Better and better," she said under her breath. "I'm going to sit down now."

"Wait. I'm starved. Do you think Lady Penelope will mind if we raid the kitchen?"

Trust the man to drop a bombshell in her lap and think

of his stomach. "I doubt it but let's go over to the cottage. It has its own kitchen."

"What cottage?" Riordan asked. He stood up and winced. After so many hours sitting at the table, his legs felt like needles were driving through them.

"If you'd stuck your head out of here, you would have found out. Come on, let's go."

"Take it easy. I'm not as young as I used to be."

"That won't save you. I want the whole story and I want it now. Everything you should have told me right at the beginning. When I think how dumb I was, waltzing into your office, trusting you—"

"Whoa," Riordan said. "You *can* trust me. We're in this together."

She cast him a sharp look and tightened her hold on his arm, tugging him along. "You, me, and your brother?"

"Well, no, but—"

"Forget it. I'll fix you something to eat and I'll fill you in on what's been happening, but then it's your turn. You've got to come straight, Riordan, or our little partnership is over. Hassan sent me after the scroll, he didn't send you. He wanted me to be the agent for its sale and that's exactly what I'm going to be unless you can give me a damn good reason why I shouldn't."

"All right," he said, surprising her by his mildness. "Food first and I want to know what's been going on, but then I'll tell you everything. Or at least as much as I know so far."

She looked at him sideways. He was worn out, there were dark shadows under his eyes and the lines around his mouth looked as though they'd been carved with a hammer. So why did just being close to him make her pulse pound?

"No tricks," she said.

"Scout's honor. How are you at omelets?"

"Middling."

They reached the cottage. Riordan stepped in after Jocelyn and looked around.

"Nice," he said.

"There are some clean clothes and toiletries for you in the second bedroom."

He ran a hand over his jaw. "If I had any class, I'd do something about that."

"You look fine." Damn the man. She turned her back on him and headed for the kitchen.

"Listen up because I'm going to do this fast. Jamal is going to England. He'll be living with friends of the Hargreaves in Surrey. He's tremendously excited. After he got that taken care of, Sir David checked out Hassan. He was a money mover but pretty up-front for all that. Our host doesn't think he was likely to be dealing in stolen goods."

Riordan made an equivocal sound and looked at the eggs she was beating in a glass bowl. "Can I have cheese with that?"

"Fine. Now it's your turn."

He settled on a stool beside the counter where she was working. His shoulders sagged and he looked done in but she refused to be swayed.

"When did you find out about the cylinder?"

His voice was husky, from fatigue or remembered emotion or both, she couldn't tell. "The day before you came to see me. I got a phone call from my brother saying that he was in New York and wanted to get together. We met at St. Patrick's Cathedral."

"Cozy," Jocelyn murmured.

"Brendan and I don't have a close relationship. We hadn't seen each other in more than four years, and we hardly ever correspond, so I was surprised to hear from him."

"What did he want?"

"He fed me a cock-and-bull story about a first-century Aramaic scroll that had been stolen from the Vatican archives and—"

"I knew it," Jocelyn broke in. "The Vatican authorities are going to try to make a claim that the scroll is rightly theirs. Why? So they can bury it for another nine centuries?"

"You're jumping ahead. Let's take one thing at a time. Brendan said he thought the scroll might be brought to me for authentication."

"What was cock-and-bull about that? I did bring it to you or at least a photocopy of part of it."

"The thing was Brendan claimed the scroll was of no particular importance. He said the only reason anybody at the Vatican cared was because the breach in security set a bad precedent. Other people might get the idea the place was ripe for the taking, that's all."

"Baloney."

"Exactly, so I knew something was up and the next day you walked in with the photocopy. One thing led to another, Saleem got garroted, and I figured we'd better join forces."

"So you could help your brother."

"No," he said patiently, "so I could get to the bottom of whatever is really going on."

She tipped the eggs into the skillet, swooshed them around, and threw in a handful of grated cheese. "And what's that?"

"I don't know," he admitted. "The scroll is difficult to read. Saleem photocopied one of the more legible portions which makes sense; I would have done the same. But the rest is faded enough to make it slow going."

"But you can read it?" Jocelyn asked.

"Oh, yeah, I can read it, it just takes time. What I know so far is that it's the account of a journey taken in Galilee in the company of several people, all followers of an itinerant rabbi named Yeshua."

"Then it has nothing to do with Jesus?" Jocelyn said. She couldn't conceal her disappointment.

"Jesus is a Greek name. None of his contemporaries called him that. To them, he was Yeshua which meant savior. Who knows what name he was actually given when he was born. Maybe that was it, if his mother was really thinking ahead, and maybe it wasn't. There's no way to tell. The account is consistent with the idea that this was the man we call Jesus traveling around with some of his followers, including the person who later wrote about their journey."

"And who was that?"

"No question there. 'I, Mary,' she calls herself. And just so there won't be any confusion, she adds, 'of the temple tower' which throws an interesting light on the whole business. Some people translate Magdalen as sorrowful or believe it refers to a town called Magdala, but it also can be translated as temple tower. 'I, Mary, of the temple tower.' Mary Magdalen."

"You're telling me she came from a temple? Then why do most people think she was a whore?"

"Because a whole lot happened between then and now. There are strong indications that some things were just plain twisted. The New Testament talks about how Mary

Magdalen had seven devils cast out of her. It doesn't actually say Jesus did it, only that it happened. We know there was an ancient ritual drama that involved the casting out of seven devils from a priestess representing the deity the ancient Semites called Mari-El, or the Female-Male creator of life. Maybe the woman we call Mary Magdalen had something to do with that. The New Testament also says there were other women involved who had evil spirits cast out and who together supported Jesus, so it sounds as though Mary Magdalen wasn't on her own. She was part of a group of women, maybe their leader."

"You've lost me. You're saying she came from a temple and was some kind of priestess?"

"I'm saying we don't know and we may never but it's still interesting to think about. The point is, if anything's every going to be found that can be called the Magdalen Scroll, it looks like we've got it."

"Is it authentic?" Jocelyn asked and held her breath.

"I can't be one hundred percent sure without further study but if I had to bet, I'd say yes."

"Whoo-ee."

"Exactly. Now can I have that omelet?"

"Oh, yeah, sure. Here." She dropped the omelet onto a plate and slid it across the counter to him. "What else have you found out?"

"Anything to drink?"

"Beer all right?"

"Perfect. This is good. I didn't know you could cook."

"There's a whole lot you don't know about me," she said just because it was too good an opportunity to pass up. "That's it so far?"

"Just about. As I said, it's slow going. But I'll tell you one thing, I did take a quick look toward the end and I've got the feeling it breaks off all of a sudden. Also, the way it starts, even though she gives her name, there's too much she doesn't say, like how she met this Yeshua. She goes right into the trip even though it seems to have occurred some time after she became one of his supporters."

"What does that mean?"

"Just that we may be dealing with a partial."

"A partial? You mean there's more?"

"I mean there may have been originally. My guess is this is only a fragment of a much more extensive work. That's a significant complication if it's true, but for the moment let's just worry about what we've actually got."

"What's the next step?" Jocelyn asked.

"First, I get some sleep. I can't even see straight at this point. Then I get back to work. I want to finish the translation before we do anything else. I figure I need a few more days to at least rough it out."

"And then?"

"Then we talk. We still don't know for sure that we're dealing with an authentic first-century document and we've got conflicting claims of ownership. On the one hand, we've got my brother claiming the scroll was stolen from the Vatican archives no less and on the other we've got Saleem who claimed to have a legal right to sell it. Those are irreconcilable claims."

"Which will have to be reconciled one way or another."

"I agree. However, you've got to keep in mind that my brother's claim that the scroll was in the possession of the Vatican is consistent with di Costello's story about it being taken back to Rome under guard."

"Di Costello said a lot of things including that the Khalduns were all killed when the scroll was stolen. Nine centuries don't make murder or theft any more palatable than if they were happening today, or at least they shouldn't."

"You realize none of that would matter in a court of law?"

"Of course not, but there are moral considerations that endure no matter how inconvenient they may become."

He didn't argue with her but he didn't agree either. Instead, he finished the omelet, thanked her again for fixing it, and took his plate over to the sink.

"I'm bushed," he said gently. They were standing close together. She could see the slow rise and fall of his breathing and was suddenly very conscious of how alone they were.

"Go to bed," she said and hoped she didn't sound as wistful as she felt.

He smiled ruefully, touched a hand to her cheek, and said, "I'm glad you're here."

"Because I make such great omelets?"

"No."

"Go to bed," she said again.

"Do I have a choice?"

"No."

"Has anyone ever told you that you tend to be just a bit negative?"

"Yes."

He laughed and dropped his hand. At the kitchen door he said, "By the way, not all the Khalduns were killed when the scroll was stolen. Di Costello says he saved the life of the eldest son. What do you suppose happened to him?"

"I have no idea."

"Neither do I but I do know memories tend to run

deep in that part of the world and nothing ever seems to be really settled."

He went off, pleased with the suggestion he'd planted, and presently she heard him getting into bed. The springs creaked once or twice and were silent.

She remembered then that he'd always been able to drop off at a moment's notice, unlike Jocelyn herself who spent the remainder of the night hovering between dreams and consciousness.

Night flowers were blooming outside her bedroom window. Either that or someone was burning incense, and there was chanting, a great deal of it, in a cavernous space where the voices resonated like deep flowing currents, and there was a man, long-boned with close-cropped hair and shining eyes who stood with his arms upraised as his bloodless lips shaped her name.

17

"Jocelyn Merriman has not contacted her office in New York since shortly after her arrival," Monsignor Ricci said. "Her employer is most concerned."

Brendan sighed and ran a hand over his eyes in a gesture his brother—and Jocelyn too—would have recognized. "I know that."

"I know that you know it," Ricci replied. He sat behind his marble and gilt desk, hands folded on its surface, and regarded his unwilling guest.

It was mid-afternoon. The heat had finally brought torrents of rain that lashed the Holy City and turned the sky yellow gray. There was an excess of electricity in the air that set everyone's nerves on edge.

"What I want to know," Ricci continued, "is whether or not you are doing anything about it."

Brendan faced his provoker—tormentor would have been giving Ricci too much credit—imperturbably. "You said a week. I still have five days."

"They will pass rapidly. Have you made any progress at all?"

"Some. My brother entered Italy four days ago by direct flight from New York. He went immediately to the Grand Hotel where he inquired as to the whereabouts of Miss Merriman. While he was in the process of doing that, she returned and they went to her room. They left the hotel together the following morning and returned in the afternoon. Several hours later, they left again and this time they did not return. No one at the Grand has seen them since. At my request, Miss Merriman's room was checked. All her luggage appears to be there as does Riordan's."

"And what conclusion does all this lead you to?" Ricci asked.

"That our suspicions were correct. Miss Merriman's visit to San Crisogono was more than the idle interest of a tourist. The boy Jamal, whom she questioned the good sister about, has something to do with the scroll. Incidentally, he, too, seems to have disappeared."

"And—"

"And that strongly suggests that my brother is in possession of the scroll, as we have already discussed. We find him, we find the scroll."

"But you are no closer to doing that," Ricci said. "All you have told me is what we already knew. Italy is a large country, they could be anywhere. Or they may have left already."

"If they had left, there would be a record and there is none. No, they're still here. Riordan would be anxious to examine the scroll. He would need a quiet place to work undisturbed. That leaves out a hotel, especially in a large city. My guess is that he has gone to ground somewhere. The only question is where."

"The *only* question? How simple you make it sound but in fact you have no idea where he has gone, do you? He could be in a hundred different places."

"I am taking steps to locate him," Brendan said quietly. He refused to give Ricci the reaction he so obviously wanted, namely anger. Indeed, he refused to give the Monsignor anything more than he already had.

"The longer I sit here talking," Brendan said, "the longer it will take me to find Riordan."

Ricci frowned, as much at the insubordination as at the truth of the statement. "Then go, but the next time we speak, I expect some evidence that you are doing your job."

Brendan resisted the urge to tell him that with any luck at all, there wouldn't be a next time. As soon as he possibly could, he was going to take an end run around the Monsignor. But first he had to find Riordan.

He left the office with his face resolutely blank and his mind in turmoil. Forget his brother and whatever he might be up to. At the moment, the ball was in Miss Jocelyn Merriman's court.

The problem was that she had no way of knowing it. In her ignorance, she could very easily make a wrong move.

He avoided his own office and decided to walk instead, finding himself eventually in one of the long galleries that filled the Vatican palaces like passages through a honeycomb. Some were open to the public but there were few members of it in evidence, discouraged as they were by the weather.

He had the Etruscan exhibits to himself. Wandering among them, he thought back to Riordan's only previous trip to Rome since Brendan had been assigned there. They had spent a few hours together with Brendan playing guide on a blazing hot summer day completely unlike the present one.

He smiled as he remembered how self-consciously proud he had felt showing his brother around the fabled Vatican. Riordan had been polite but had made no pretense of feeling any attachment to the place. To him, it was simply a cluster of museums, interesting in themselves but without greater significance.

Riordan had spent only a day or two in Rome on that visit. He'd been going on to Greece for some dig or other. Some dig—There'd been a write-up on it a few months later in the *International Herald Tribune*. Some mention of—

He couldn't place it and the harder he tried, the further the memory retreated. After a while, he gave it up and walked back to his office. He sat down behind his desk, pulled out a folder of material requiring his attention, and resigned himself to a long night.

While rain pelted Rome, Sardinia basked in sun. Jocelyn lay by the pool and tried not to feel ungrateful. Sir David had taken Jamal to the mainland to start the boy on his trip to England. Lady Penelope was in the greenhouse doing something or other with orchids. Riordan was where he had been almost continuously except for a few hours sleep at the cottage. He had gone back to the library before dawn and hadn't been seen since.

Jocelyn itched to go after him but stopped herself. The work he was doing, picking his way through the maze of an ancient language whose meanings were lost or at least obscured, demanded total concentration. She could help best by staying away.

Which left her with nothing to do except relax. Reading kept her busy for a while, doing laps in the pool helped, but eventually she had to face facts, she just wasn't any good at doing nothing.

She thought about going for a walk but the heat haze rising from the road derailed that idea. She could take a nap but then she wouldn't be able to sleep at night and besides, she wasn't tired.

Or she could take care of a little business. Her conscience had been tweaking her, knowing as she did that Wilbur would be worrying. She had deliberately misled him about the contents of Saleem's note, and she had made no effort to keep him up to date with events. She really ought to rectify that.

There was a phone in the cottage. She dialed the international operator, gave her credit card number along with her number at Holcroft & Farnsworth, and waited. Several moments passed before Trey answered.

"Well, hi," he said. "How's Rome?"

"Fine." No sense getting bogged down in unnecessary detail such as where she actually was. "Anything major happening?"

"Uh, gee, let me check. It's been pretty quiet but Mr. Holcroft has been asking for you."

Wilbur didn't often bestir himself to inquire after his employees, presuming that if they wanted to retain their prestigious and lucrative positions, they would take care of matters on their own.

"Did he call you?" she asked.

"No, he came down yesterday to see if you'd been in touch and then again this morning."

Wilbur? Left his office—twice? She really had been remiss.

"Do you know if he's in now?"

"I don't think so. He went out to lunch a while ago and I haven't seen him come back."

Wilbur lunching out was an event, especially this time of year when he despised New York and either holed up in his office or abandoned the city entirely for fairer climes. But then she remembered he'd also been out the evening she returned from seeing Saleem. Perhaps he simply wasn't as reclusive as he liked to appear.

"I'll call back," she said. "Anything else?"

"Not really. Oh, wait. Somebody named Fairley called. He said he was with the police department and wanted to chat with you."

Jocelyn stiffened in surprise. Clearly, the New York Police Department was better at its job than she'd thought, or at least the homicide division was. How had Fairley found her?

"Did he leave a number?"

"Yep, I've got it here someplace. Say, is anything going on?"

And people claimed an Ivy League education wasn't what it used to be. Nothing got past this guy.

"I'll fill you in later," Jocelyn said. "Tell Mr. Holcroft I called, everything is fine, and I'll be in touch. Also, if Detective Fairley calls again, tell him I'm out of the country and ask why he wants to talk with me."

"Okay," Trey said, ever obliging.

Fairley would love being grilled by him, Jocelyn thought. "Miss Merriman is abroad. Does she know what this is in reference to?"

Miss Merriman most certainly did but she wasn't about

to admit it, especially not by returning Fairley's call. Not yet anyway. Whatever he wanted to ask her would have to wait.

She hung up a few minutes later and sat staring at the wall, trying to decide what to do next. Almost on an afterthought, she dialed again, this time calling her own apartment. She'd left her answering machine on. A tone from the beeper she carried in her purse triggered it to play her messages.

There were three. Her dry cleaner had called to say they'd found her blue silk blouse. The chairman of her building committee wanted to know if she could help with fund-raising for the annual block party. And Father Brendan Nolan wanted to hear from her. He had left both a number and a time for her to call.

Jocelyn set down the phone, noticing in passing that her hand shook. A host of questions flooded through her. How did he know about her? Had Riordan told him?

If so, then he had to have been in contact with his brother since their meeting in the Cathedral even though he had said otherwise. She didn't want to believe Riordan was lying, but if the information hadn't come from him, then who had provided it?

It was already later than the time he had said to call but she tried the number anyway. It had a Roman prefix and belonged to an osteria that, judging by the noise in the background, was doing a brisk business.

She hung up without asking for Father Nolan. Why hadn't he given her a number at the Vatican? Was it possible he was acting privately, without authorization, and if so, what exactly had he taken it upon himself to do?

The image of the black car careening out of the narrow

street darted through her mind. She thought of Saleem and shivered.

The remainder of the afternoon passed quietly. When the worst of the heat was done, Lady Penelope suggested they drive into the village. While she picked up a few groceries, Jocelyn found a hole-in-the wall clothing store where she bought herself a couple of simple linen dresses and a pair of sandals. She liked Lady Penelope and enjoyed being with her, but the waiting remained hard.

It continued through the evening. Sir David returned after getting Jamal safely off. He reported the boy was dazed but happy, clutching his brand new British passport, the existence of which Sir David did not bother to explain.

"Do you think we should ask Riordan to join us?" Lady Penelope asked as they were sitting down to dinner.

Sir David shook his head. "Remember how he was in Greece. He'd go to ground with a problem and come back several days later with the solution. Best to leave him to it now."

"He is making progress," Jocelyn said. She didn't want to steal any of Riordan's thunder but she thought their host and hostess were entitled to know what they had gotten themselves into. "There's a good chance this could be the Magdalen Scroll."

Lady Penelope paused with her fork in midair and stared at her. "You mean it was actually written by Mary Magdalen?"

"So it seems."

"How extraordinary. Documents left by women are so scarce. A few diaries, a handful of household accounts, but nothing so old or so important. However did she manage it?"

"She refers to herself as being associated with a temple," Jocelyn said, "which could provide a clue. She may have been part of a group of women who dedicated their lives to their faith. Without the distraction of husbands and children, they could have become better educated."

"Wasn't there some business a few years ago about a woman possibly being the author of parts of the Old Testament?" Sir David asked.

Jocelyn nodded. "That was speculation based on subtle literary analysis. It set off a fire storm among religious scholars."

"As this undoubtedly will," Lady Penelope said. "No wonder Riordan wants to keep it under wraps until he's really sure of what it is."

"There's an added complication," Jocelyn said. "The Vatican may be prepared to claim that the scroll is church property. They could sue for its return and also block publication of either the contents or a translation."

"Wouldn't that only succeed in drawing even more attention to the scroll?" Sir David asked. "I imagine they'd want to keep it as quiet as possible."

Jocelyn thought of Brendan Nolan's call. "Perhaps," she said noncommittally and turned her attention back to her food.

She was lying in bed hours later when Riordan finally returned to the cottage. She heard him moving around in the kitchen for a few moments, then there was silence.

Jocelyn hesitated. He was a grown man long accustomed to looking after himself. The attraction between them was a complication she didn't need. She should stay right where she was, mind her own business, and wait until morning to tackle him on such matters as the scroll, his brother, and whatever might lie between the two.

But the silence had come too soon, there hadn't been time for him to fix himself anything decent to eat. And she could hear nothing to indicate that he was heading for bed.

Slowly, she got up and pulled on her robe. She had shut the bedroom door. When she opened it, she saw only a sliver of light coming from the kitchen area.

Riordan was sitting at the counter with his head in his hands. There was no sign of any food. She was next to him before he realized she was there.

"It's okay," she said when he looked up, "I just wanted to make sure you were all right."

He blinked as though to clear his vision. "I'm fine, just a little frayed around the edges." Which was putting it mildly. His words were slurred with fatigue, his eyes were red-rimmed, and his normally healthy color had been reduced to an exhausted pallor.

"You're pushing yourself too hard," she said.

He shrugged. "We can't hole up here forever. I've got to get this done."

"You will but you don't have to wear yourself out in the process." She paused, acutely aware of how he was making her feel. When she'd known him before, she'd been so much younger and everything had seemed so much simpler. Now the stakes were higher than she had ever imagined and she had no chance at all of walking away from them.

In such circumstances, she usually took refuge in the safely ordinary. "Do you want something to eat?"

He shook his head. "I'm too tired, but thanks."

She looked at him, slumped on the stool, his head drifting toward the counter, and sighed. "You can't sleep here."

"Wanna bet?"

"Come on." Gently, she took his arm. He leaned on her as she steered him toward his room. The bed was still unmade from the morning. She straightened the sheets quickly and fluffed the pillows. "Sit down."

He did, looking at her bemusedly. "I like your hair down. Makes you look more like the Josie I remember."

"Don't get nostalgic on me, Riordan. That was a long time ago."

"You're kidding? It was the blink of an eye, less than a fragment of a cosmic moment, not even a ripple in the eons of time."

"Right. Take off your shoes."

He obliged and smiled at her. "You haven't changed as much as you think."

"Wanna bet?"

"Sure. Oh, you decked yourself out to get what you wanted but you're still the same person inside."

"Little Josie Mulkowsky from Ozone Park, Queens?"

"The one, the only."

She put her hands on his shoulders and pushed. He landed on his back on the bed. "I've got news for you, Riordan. Josie Mulkowsky is long gone. You can't pick who you're born but you can sure decide who you'll be."

His brow furrowed. "That sounds like something out of a greeting card."

"Who asked you anyway? Go to sleep."

"Wait a minute." He reached out, snagging her hand. "I didn't mean to make you mad."

"You didn't. Good night."

"Yeah, I did. I'm sorry. It's just that—"

"What?"

"Josie Mulkowsky was a nice person. So what that she came from Ozone Park? She was smart, funny, beautiful, and she had a lot of guts. I was crazy about her."

"Crazy enough to walk away."

"Hey, I said *you* had guts. I didn't say I had any. You scared the daylights out of me. I looked at you, I saw all kinds of things—commitment, responsibility, the whole ball of wax."

Her smile was the kind martinis could be chilled on. "You want to take a guess how many men over how many centuries have used that excuse? 'I meant well, babe, I was just kind of overwhelmed. Not my fault you're so much woman.' You know how that sounds, Riordan?"

His eyes opened a little wider. He seemed to be waking up some. "I'm getting the idea."

"It sounds like crap. Grade-A, extra prime, top-of-the-line crap. I'm surprised at you."

He looked at her sheepishly. "I'm not at my best. 'I, Mary' may have had a lot going for her but her penmanship needed work."

"You're changing the subject. You want to get me asking you about the scroll but I'm not going to do it. I'm going to bed."

"Sounds good to me."

That surprised her but what the heck, if he wanted to play it that way, she didn't care. Her feelings weren't involved at all. She was impervious. He was a part of her past, over and done with.

"Speaking of Grade-A crapola," Riordan said.

"What're you, some kind of mind reader?"

"Only with you, sweetheart," he said and gently tugged her down onto the bed.

18

She remembered how it had been between them all those years ago, having no choice but to remember it, and she knew it had not been like this.

Then it had been beautiful, tender, moving, lit by the steady confidence of youth and spirits as yet undaunted by disappointment. She could shut her eyes and recall it all exactly, caught at the very moment when nothing would ever be quite the same.

All these years she had been changing, never absolutely sure into what, and now she was finding out.

It helped that they were both nervous. He had trouble undoing the knot in her belt, she snagged the zipper of his fly. They fell across the bed, sending the springs to creaking wildly.

"We're so cool," Riordan said, grinning.

"It's all that clean living."

"This thing's locked, definitely."

"Speaking of locked."

"Oohh, watch it. I'll do that."

He did, she did, skin touched skin, hot, smooth, need-ing. She shut her eyes against the wave of sensation, opening them to find herself gazing up at him, hard and strong above her, waiting.

"Jocelyn, this time . . ."

She nodded, savoring the weight of him, wanting so much. Her hands ran over the taut skin, the clenched muscles, claiming him. "This time . . . let's try, all right?"

He nodded once, acknowledgment of what they both knew: They were past the point of false promises or easy assurances. They had this time, this precious now. Tomor-row they might have nothing—or everything. But now, right now—

His mouth took hers in an instant, unstinting in its de-mand. She gasped, her breath lost in him, and lifted her hips. Later perhaps, there might, if they were lucky, be time for so much else but now there was only the surge of their bodies, moving in instinctive memory and the sweet, hot rush of relief when they were joined.

She felt him deep within her and almost sobbed from the beauty of it, the sense of his strength given to her, cherished. Then he was moving, deeply and rhythmically, and she with him, higher and higher, until aloneness dis-solved, separateness vanished, and they were, as they had briefly glimpsed in that long ago, whole.

They lay for a long time afterward, holding onto each other, not sleeping but drifting from dream to wakeful-ness until the cock strutting in the garden crowed to sum-mon them to a new day.

*   *   *

"Nice dress," Riordan said. It was the next morning. They were having breakfast alone in the cottage, munching on fresh oranges and muffins culled from the freezer.

The dress in question was lying across the back of a chair, Jocelyn not having gotten around to putting it on yet. It was one of those she had bought the previous day.

"Mind if I have it?" Riordan asked.

She looked at him levelly. "Is this your way of telling me something kinky?"

"Afraid not. I need some linen for a little experiment. That looks as though it would fit the bill."

"All right," Jocelyn said. The dress hadn't cost much, she didn't mind sacrificing it, but she was curious as to what he was up to.

"Why linen?" she asked.

"The scroll is linen. I want to get a better idea of how hard it is to write on."

"It would be slow going, wouldn't it, harder than with papyrus or vellum?"

"Probably but it may have been all Mary had available. Anyway, I want to give it a try."

"Have you made any more progress with the translation?"

He nodded. "Some. Mostly she's talking about a trip around Galilee with Yeshua preaching to several different groups of people. At one point, they stayed at the house of the man named Uriel which is the part that was on the photocopy. The interesting thing is that this is all new material; so far as I know there's no mention of such a visit in any of the other testaments."

"Any idea why not?"

"Not so far. She says the other disciples were with

them so they could have written about it if they'd wanted to."

"Wait a minute, what do you mean 'other'?"

Riordan grinned. He sat cross-legged on the bed, unabashedly naked, and reached for another muffin. "Picked up on that, did you? She uses the same word to describe herself as she does to describe the men we've come to know as the disciples. The problem is that the word can be translated different ways. It can mean follower, or pupil, or devotee, or disciple. It all depends on how you interpret it. Frankly, she doesn't seem to have considered the issue to be very important. Either that or she deliberately fudged it."

"I don't get it," Jocelyn said. "I expected you to discover that Mary Magdalen flat-out called herself a disciple of Christ. That would go a long way toward explaining why the church suppressed the scroll. But instead you're saying it's open to interpretation?"

"That's right. Maybe she was and maybe she wasn't. At least that's what I can tell so far."

"There has to be more then."

"Possibly. I won't find it sitting here." Yet he made no effort to move. On the contrary, his eyes wandered over her with unabashed appreciation until she flushed warmly which in turn made him laugh.

They fell together in a wealth of crumbs, the oranges bouncing off the bed to roll across the floor, where several hours later they were at last retrieved.

The osteria was a working man's place popular with laborers, taxi drivers, and underpaid clerks from the nearby offices. An occasional tourist wandered in but few stayed. The ancient wooden floors smelled of old wine, the tables were scarred, and the food, while edible, was plain and rough.

Brendan sat toward the back. He had a glass of Chianti in front of him and a plate of bread and sausage, but he had touched none of it. He wore civilian clothes, having left his cassock behind. His eyes did not stray far from the phone.

At five minutes before 2:00 P.M., he stood up and leaned against the wall next to the booth, arms folded over his chest, waiting. It was the third day he had done this. On the previous two days, nothing had happened. The proprietor, working behind the counter, frowned slightly but said nothing.

The phone rang. Brendan picked it up before the sound died. He spoke briskly.

"Yes?"

A woman's voice replied. It was cool, distant, and wary. "Am I speaking with Father Brendan Nolan?"

He resisted the impulse to sag in relief and said, "That's right. Miss Merriman?"

"How do you know Wilbur Holcroft?"

Apparently, they were not going to waste any time on pleasantries.

"What makes you ask that?"

"I've thought about it. Wilbur is the only person who could have told you that I was looking for the scroll."

Brendan sighed. Gently, he said, "I am a priest. My job is to counsel those in distress. Mr. Holcroft is concerned about his future."

There was silence for a moment as she digested this. "Why would he be concerned? The firm is doing very well."

She sounded genuinely puzzled. It never failed to

amaze Brendan how perfectly intelligent people managed
to ignore the fact of their own mortality.

"He is in his seventies, Miss Merriman. Shall we say he
is looking ahead?"

"I see." Her disgust was plain. "Wilbur's decided he's
scared of dying so he turned to the church for help and
you blackmailed him into helping you instead. Tell me,
did you offer to sell him a few indulgences while you were
at it?"

Brendan closed his eyes for a moment, fighting for patience. It had always been his weak point. He had lost
count of all the hours he had spent on his knees praying
for the grace of forbearance.

"No one blackmailed him, Miss Merriman. He offered
his assistance. He was concerned that the firm's reputation would suffer if it became involved with stolen property."

"Really? That isn't what he told me. I wouldn't place
any bets on who contacted whom to start with but that's
neither here nor there. In case you haven't noticed, Wilbur isn't exactly up-to-date."

"You've shut him out very thoroughly, Miss Merriman,
beginning with the red herring of San Constanza instead
of San Crisogono."

He let that sink in for a moment before adding, "Yes,
we know about where you really went and we know it's
likely that your quest has been successful, that you and
Riordan are in possession of the scroll."

"Would that be the worthless first-century scroll the
Vatican really wasn't concerned about losing?"

"Just so that we understand each other, Miss Merriman, I don't enjoy lying. The fact is I really do believe it's
a sin. But I am more concerned about protecting my

brother. You are both involved in a matter you don't understand and which can lead you into serious trouble."

"You mean the kind of trouble that happened to Hassan Saleem?"

"Who?"

"I really don't think we have anything to say to each other."

"Wait a moment. I don't know who you're talking about, but I do know that you and my brother are involved in a matter that could turn very ugly very quickly. You must tell me where you are. We must meet to discuss all this."

He waited, the phone clasped to his ear, but the only sound that reached him was a soft click as the connection was broken.

Jocelyn's hand was shaking as she hung up. The experience of talking with Riordan's brother had upset her more than she could have anticipated. It would have been so easy to trust him, to respond to the worry that was so evident in every word he said.

Only one thing had stopped her, the claim that he didn't know about Hassan. Brendan Nolan was at the center of the Vatican's efforts to reclaim the scroll. She couldn't believe he was ignorant of the fate of the man who so briefly possessed it.

She sat for a time trying to decide what to do before rousing herself to go back outside. Riordan was in the library. She looked in on him, finding him immersed in work, and was about to withdraw when he glanced up and saw her. The smile that touched his face found its match in her own.

"Hi," he said and held out a hand.

She went to him, fingers curling around his.

He pointed to the pile of handwritten sheets covered with neatly printed lettering in two alphabets. "I think it's starting to come together."

She was glad to hear it but she was more intrigued by what had happened to her dress. It lay on the table, cut into strips. A small, separate piece showed splotches of ink.

"Is this the experiment?" she asked.

He nodded. "You were right, it's hard to write on but it is possible if you go slowly. The problem is getting the ink to fix."

"Would Mary have been able to overcome that?"

"Obviously, she did. The cloth itself may have been treated in some way or she could have used an ink I'm not familiar with."

She looked down at the pages of closely written notes and thought of the long hours he had struggled to comprehend the message of a woman dead now for almost two millennia.

"You can't work all the time," she said. "Come for a swim."

She expected him to argue and added quickly, "Sir David and Lady Penelope have gone out."

His smile deepened. "Why do you suppose they did that."

"I think they believe we could use some time alone."

"Perceptive people, the Hargreaves," he said and went with her.

They swam naked in the pool, playing like children until the play turned serious. He lifted her out, the water running in rivulets down their bodies. Carrying her, he walked into the shadowy quiet of the cottage.

19

Jocelyn woke once in the night and reached out a hand, seeking Riordan. The other side of the bed was empty. She sighed, turned over, and drifted back to sleep.

Lady Penelope was on the patio when Jocelyn emerged early the next morning. She was clipping roses and humming to herself. "There you are," she said. "We've had news of Jamal. He's in Surrey and everything is fine."

"Wonderful. May I help you with that?"

"Thanks but it's done. Do you think Riordan will be wanting breakfast?"

"I haven't seen him but I can try to find out."

"He's in the library. I took him a pot of tea hours ago. Doesn't he ever sleep?"

"I think he's anxious to finish."

"I'm sure he is. Come on then, let's see what we can put together."

She led the way into the kitchen where they found Sir David slicing ham and generally making himself useful.

"My turn to cook," he said. "Go away. I'll call you when it's done."

"Oh, dear," Lady Penelope murmured when they were out of earshot, "whenever he gets like this, it takes days to find anything."

"It does smell delicious in there."

"Oh, David is quite a good cook. Ever since he gave up those dreadful cigars, he's actually been able to taste food. Some of the combinations he puts together I'd never think of but I never turn them down either."

"You've been married a long time, haven't you?" Jocelyn asked.

Lady Penelope nodded. "Forty-five years next autumn. I can't believe it's been anywhere near that long."

"It must be wonderful when you can feel so secure with each other, so settled."

The older woman raised a graceful eyebrow. "My dear, is that how you imagine it's been? Good heavens, I don't suppose I've had a settled day since I stepped down the aisle. If that's what I'd wanted, I would have married Willy Forbisher and been done with it."

"Who was Willy Forbisher?" Jocelyn asked with a smile.

"David's rival for my affections. A dear man who became head of the royal arts council, spent two months a year in Bermuda, and raised splendid spaniels. Also, never touched a cigar so far as I know. He died quite suddenly of heart failure ten years ago having led an exemplary and utterly uneventful life."

"It doesn't sound as though you're riddled with regrets."

"I'm sorry Willy died. I liked him but I wanted a good deal more. With David, I never quite knew what would be happening or why, but I was always certain it wouldn't be boring."

Jocelyn laughed. "I have to admit that's as good a prescription for marriage as I've heard."

"Hmmm, I rather thought you'd feel that way." She touched a hand to a pale yellow rose blossom and smiled. "Shall we see if Riordan wants to join us?"

"I'll go," Jocelyn said. She left the patio and walked the short distance to the library, entering by the outside door. Riordan was standing beside the table. The strips of linen were set out in front of him. He was folding them as she entered.

"Lady Penelope wants to know if you'd like some breakfast."

"As a matter of fact, I would." He touched his mouth lightly to hers. His eyes were possessive as they scanned her. "How did you sleep?"

"Like a baby. Ever think of trying it?"

He laughed softly. "Maybe when this is over but I will take you up on breakfast. What's that I smell?"

"I'm not sure. Sir David is cooking." She glanced at the table. "Are you getting any closer?"

"To putting it together? I think so. Mary had a good head for detail. For instance, she says that when they came to the house of Uriel it had been freshly whitewashed, new cushions were laid on the floor, and special foods had been prepared in honor of Yeshua's visit."

"That's nice," Jocelyn said. "It's the kind of thing a woman would notice."

"So did Yeshua apparently. Mary says that he thanked Uriel and his wife for their hospitality but he also warned them not to put too much store in any one man. He said the path to God lay within each individual."

"That's an inspiring thought."

"Not if you're trying to run a church based on the idea that only a select priesthood can intercede between humanity and God. If you buy the idea that this is the personal testament of Mary Magdalen and that she accurately recorded statements made by the teacher called Yeshua—Savior—then you have to question the very concept of religious authority."

"No wonder the Vatican kept it suppressed all these centuries," Jocelyn murmured. "And no wonder they want it back."

"Exactly. The question is how far will they go to get it? If what happened to Saleem is anything to judge by, the answer seems to be as far as they have to."

He shook his head wearily. "Brendan was a bright kid, stubborn as hell but without a mean streak in him. What the hell happened?"

"Don't jump the gun," Jocelyn said gently. "We don't know how much he knows. Besides, he's still your brother and whatever differences there are between you, he's worried about your safety."

"What makes you think that?"

She took a deep breath and looked at him squarely. "He knows about me, Riordan. He found out from Wilbur Holcroft. I called the answering machine at my apartment. There was a message from your brother. I talked with him yesterday afternoon."

He stared at her dumbfounded. "Why didn't you tell me?"

"Because you didn't need something more to worry about. Besides, it didn't amount to anything. He does know that we have the scroll but that wasn't exactly a surprise. He wants us to return it."

"That's all he said, that we should give it back?"

"He said things could get ugly."

"That's news?"

She hesitated, reluctant to drag in all her suspicions, but finally she said, "He claimed not to know anything about Saleem."

"And you believed him?" Riordan demanded.

"Not exactly, but I thought you might."

He made an exasperated sound. "Did you tell him where we were?"

"Of course not! I didn't tell Wilbur either although he's undoubtedly trying to find out."

"You get a call from my brother, call him back right at the heart of the Vatican, and have a nice little chat about returning the scroll. Have I got that?"

"Not really. The number he left for me wasn't at the Vatican. It was an osteria somewhere in Rome."

Riordan's brow creased. "He had you call a wineshop instead of his office?"

"That's right. He told me what time to call and he was there waiting. I'd say he's being very cautious."

"At least that sounds like him. He was never dumb. So they know we have it?"

Jocelyn nodded. "Not only that but he knew about San Crisogono which means he had to have information from another source in addition to Wilbur. I hate to say it but I think I was followed."

"Could be. It would explain the black car and—" He broke off, his nose wrinkling. "What's that smell?"

Jocelyn became aware of it at the same time. "Something burning. Sir David must be having an off day."

"I wasn't very hungry. With a little luck I can finish up here and—Phew, that really stinks."

"It's getting worse. I'd better go see if they need any help."

"I'll come with you."

They left the library and crossed the empty patio. With each step they took, the smell became thicker and more cloying. Before they reached the kitchen, they could see thin tendrils of smoke.

"Sir David," Jocelyn called, "is everything all right?"

There was no answer. She pushed through the kitchen door. Riordan was right behind her. Abruptly, they both stopped. Sir David and Lady Penelope were sitting at the kitchen table. Behind them, smoke still rose from the cast iron skillet that had held slices of ham but the pan had been pushed off the burner and already the smell was beginning to ease.

Near the stove, facing the door, was Brendan.

Jocelyn blinked once, twice, doubting the evidence of her own eyes. Riordan had warned her but she still wasn't prepared for this. The brothers weren't identical but they did resemble each other very strongly. Brendan was a few pounds heavier, his eyes a fraction more deeply set, and his hair more neatly trimmed. He wore a windbreaker and khaki slacks, and held an automatic pistol in his right hand.

"Shit," Riordan said.

Brendan smiled faintly. "Nice to see you, too, brother." He waved the pistol in the direction of the table. "Sit down."

Jocelyn was inclined to obey, the pistol had that effect. But Riordan ignored it. His cheeks were darkly flushed and there was a light in his eyes she had never seen before.

"You son of a bitch," he said. "You're with them all the

way. You don't give a damn about anything except making sure that nobody rocks the boat. And you call yourself a priest. You've got the nerve to—"

"Shut up," Brendan said. A nerve pulsed in his jaw. The hand holding the gun was white-knuckled. "I told you to sit down. For once in your life, you're going to listen to what I have to say."

Jocelyn stepped forward quickly and took Riordan's arm. She was trembling but managed to keep her voice steady. "Come on, there's nothing else you can do. It won't hurt to hear him out."

Riordan was unconvinced but he let her guide him over to the table. They sat down between their hosts. Closer up, Jocelyn could see the nervous flicker in Lady Penelope's eyes. Their gazes met for an instant.

"Contrary to the way this looks," Brendan said, "I'm not a fan of guns. I wouldn't have brought it except I didn't much like the idea of going up against my brother —not to mention Sir David Hargreave—unarmed."

Riordan made no response but Sir David inclined his head slightly. His eyes never left Brendan's face. "I'll take that as a compliment," he said.

"I'm not sure I mean it as one," Brendan said. "But I know about Sir David. When I realized where you were, I thought I'd better come prepared."

"How did you realize?" Riordan demanded.

"A friend in the Rome telephone bureau traced the call to the osteria."

Jocelyn paled. She had considered the possibility but had thought the risk was worthwhile.

"It was supposed to look like I was just covering my own tracks," Brendan said quietly, "which I was to a certain extent. But I figured you'd be more relaxed if you weren't calling the Vatican."

"You figured right," Jocelyn said bitterly. "I really did it, didn't I?"

"Don't blame yourself," Sir David said. "This may not be entirely unfortunate. After all, at some point the church authorities do have to be heard from. It may as well be now."

"I'm not listening to anything while there's a gun waving in my face," Riordan said.

"Stubbornness appears to run in the family," Sir David murmured. He looked at Brendan. "Why don't we dispense with the gun, Father Nolan? You really don't need it. I think I'm safe in saying you have our undivided attention."

"I need more than that," Brendan said softly. But he slid the safety back on and put the gun in the pocket of the windbreaker, out of sight though still within easy reach. "I need your cooperation."

"Fat chance," Riordan said.

"Don't be petulant," Lady Penelope chided. "Hear him out."

"It's simple," Brendan said. "The scroll has to be returned to the Vatican. It's church property, it was removed illegally, and unless it's returned at once there'll be hell to pay. Besides," he added, "there's no reason for anyone to want to keep it." He took a breath and looked at each of them. "It's a fake."

"It can't be," Jocelyn said. "It's been in the Vatican archives for almost nine hundred years."

"That's right and it's seven hundred years older than that but it's *still* a fake. It was created in the fourth century during a time of upheaval and conflict. It was a desperate attempt to prevent the emergence of a unified church. Maybe the people who did it were well-intentioned and maybe they weren't. At the least, they were horribly misguided. If they had succeeded, the result would have been chaos."

Jocelyn shook her head dazedly. "You're saying Mary Magdalen had nothing to do with it?"

"She was dead a good two hundred and fifty years before it ever came into being. I'm telling you, it's a forgery. The person who actually wrote it—whoever that was— had access to first-century Aramaic documents. Why not, there were plenty of them still around. He did a good job, I grant him that. But the whole thing is a tissue of lies."

"All that about traveling with Yeshua, the visit to Uriel's house—"

"Lies intended to undermine a confident, determined church that was about to transform the Western world."

Brendan looked at his brother. "You may disagree with some of the things that have been done in the church's name, but you can't deny that it has been a beacon of faith and hope for millions. The scroll is just one in a long and sordid history of attempts to change that. With the grace of God it didn't succeed but in the wrong hands today it could still do harm."

In the silence that followed, the four people at the table looked at each other. Jocelyn thought it was impossible to doubt Brendan's sincerity. He truly believed what he said and she couldn't help but be impressed by it herself. But her reaction was not of paramount concern. What mattered was what Riordan thought.

He sighed deeply as the anger seemed to go out of him. Softly, he said, "All right, Brendan, we've listened. Now I'd like you to return the favor. You make a persuasive case. It's logical, even believable. But what do you have to back you up? Where does your information come from?"

"It comes from the highest and most reputable sources."

"You're saying the Pope himself told you this?"

"No, of course not. The Holy Father can't be expected to concern himself with such a thing. I was briefed by His Eminence, Cardinal Pasqual Manzini, the Vatican Secretary of State. Is that a good enough authority for you?"

"It might be if Manzini was an historian or an archaeologist, but he isn't. He can't have determined for himself that the scroll is a forgery. Someone else had to do that. Who?"

"It's been recognized as a forgery for centuries," Brendan said, not hiding his irritation. "At the time it was brought back to Rome from Jerusalem, it was known to be a fake. But a dangerous one that couldn't be left lying around."

"I see," Riordan said slowly. "You believe the scroll is a forgery because Cardinal Manzini says so and he supposedly believes it because that's what's always been believed. So far I see a lot of faith and no fact."

Brendan shook his head impatiently. "This is a waste of time. How do we know anything? What you've never understood is that it always comes down to faith in the end."

"Not in a case like this. There are tests that can determine the age of the scroll."

"They're not reliable," Brendan said.

"Not to the precise year, no. But they can certainly narrow it down to first century or fourth. If the church is so convinced that the scroll is a forgery, why don't they just allow it to be tested?"

"Precisely because they are so sure. There is no reason

to publicize a recognized fake. As I said, it could still do harm."

"Why?" Riordan demanded. "Because people would feel driven to ask questions? Maybe they'd ask why a fourth-century forger setting out to undermine the authority of the church would do so in the name of a woman when a man's voice would have carried far more weight. Maybe they'd wonder why such an attempt would include only a single reference that raises questions about priestly authority instead of an entire diatribe against it. Worse yet, maybe they'd ask how the church got the scroll in the first place. Explaining all those dead Khalduns could still be awkward, not to mention Hassan Saleem."

Brendan frowned. "That's the second time that name has come up. Who is Hassan Saleem?"

"I told you," Jocelyn murmured. "He doesn't know."

Riordan looked hard at his brother. Slowly, he asked, "Is that true?"

"That I have no knowledge of someone named Hassan Saleem? Yes, it's true. Who is he?"

"Was he," Jocelyn said quietly. "He was killed in New York a few days ago, but before he died he sent me a letter that led to where he had hidden the scroll."

Brendan let out his breath slowly. His hand fell away from the windbreaker. "Who killed him?"

"There's a detective in New York named Fairley who would really like to know that. In fact, I'm supposed to call him."

"Why don't we?" Riordan asked. He stood up before anyone could object. "If nothing else, it should convince my brother that nothing is as simple as he believes."

It was late afternoon in New York. Fairley could have been a lot of places—out on a case, schmoozing with the pretty sergeant down the hall, maybe even enjoying a rare day off. But as it happened, he was at his desk. He picked up the phone.

"Yeah?"

"Detective Fairley?"

"Yeah. Who's this?"

"Jocelyn Merriman. You wanted to speak with me."

"That's right, I did. Your office said you were out of town."

"Out of the country, actually. I'm in Italy. What did you want to talk with me about?"

"The murder of Hassan Saleem. Ring a bell?"

"Yes, I'm sorry to say it does. How did you find me?"

"Witness fingered the cab driver. Took us a while to run him down. Then we had to trace your movements from where you got out of the taxi. Just for future reference, Miss Merriman, you're a good-looking woman. People tend to remember you."

"I'll keep that in mind," she said softly. "I don't know how much help I can be. I only met Mr. Saleem once, the day before he was killed."

"Yeah, you said you were casual acquaintances, I think was the way you put it. Even so, maybe you can answer a question for me?"

"I can try."

"The witness who fingered your driver happens to be a bum who hangs out across from where Saleem lived. He's not the most reliable guy in the world; fact is he seems to spend a lot of his time orbiting out near Pluto. But he was right about you so maybe he's not totally wrong on the rest."

"What rest?" Jocelyn asked. Her eyes slipped from

Riordan to Brendan. The priest's hand was back inside his windbreaker.

"He says that on the night Saleem was murdered he saw two guys in black suits go inside his building. They came out a few minutes later, one from the way he'd come in and the other from the building next door. Oh, yeah, one other thing."

"What's that?"

"He says they were both priests."

"Pri—"

"They were wearing those white collars like they do."

"Priests."

Brendan's hand was moving. The gun slid free, pointed straight at her.

"Put the phone down," he said.

20

Brendan didn't wait to see if his order was obeyed. He ran past Jocelyn, heading toward the side door that led out of the kitchen. Riordan was directly behind him. Sir David took one quick step after them and stopped. He turned and walked over to the cabinet on the far wall. He withdrew a key on a chain attached to his trousers and unlocked the cabinet. From it, he withdrew a pair of automatic pistols.

"Dear—" Lady Penelope said.

"Go into the library, both of you."

Jocelyn hesitated. There was still Fairley in New York. She put the phone back to her ear. It had gone dead. With her stomach knotting, she followed Lady Penelope.

Riordan didn't know exactly what he had in mind when he went after his brother. He was only sure that something was going terribly wrong and that Brendan, deservedly or not, was in the thick of it. Never mind that they had chosen different paths in life. When the going got this tough, Nolans stuck together. That was enough to drive him out into the merciless heat of the day.

"Brendan!"

"Over here. Keep your voice down."

"What the hell's going on?"

They crouched together in the bushes behind the kitchen. Riordan could feel his own heart beating rapidly and felt the rising flush of heat warming his skin. His mouth was dry. His hands flexed and unflexed, wanting a weapon. Old memories, deliberately suppressed, stirred and groaned.

"I saw something in the bushes behind the house," Brendan said, his voice low and harsh. "Someone. Who's supposed to be around here?"

Riordan swallowed hard. "No one. The Hargreaves gave their servants some time off."

"Anybody else who might come by?"

"I doubt it. The house can't even be seen from the road so a hiker or some other tourist isn't likely to drop in."

Brendan tensed. He raised a hand, silencing him. Nearby, they heard the rustle of something large moving. Riordan took a breath and raised his head slightly. A shape appeared around a corner of the house, then another. Two men.

"Give me the gun," Riordan said.

Brendan shook his head. "This isn't your fight."

"Bullshit. It's been my fight all along. Besides, I know a little more about this kind of thing than you do."

Brendan hesitated. He was clearly torn between the need for help and the desire to shoulder the burden alone. Finally, he said, "What will you do?"

"Whatever I have to. Give me the gun."

"These men . . . God forgive them but they may be killers."

Riordan's smile was cold and deadly. It caught Brendan's breath in his throat and locked it there. "You know something, brother? I already figured that out."

He reached out and took the gun from Brendan. Riordan checked the safety and finding it still on, grimaced. He corrected that before lifting his head again for a quick look around. Seeing nothing, he said, "Stay here."

"Where are you going?"

"To reconnoiter. I want to find out for sure how many there are and what they're carrying."

Before Brendan could object, Riordan slipped away into the shadows around the house. He moved quickly and silently. Old skills, acid-etched, resurfaced. He ran with his body tucked into a crouch. His breath was steady and his heartbeat had returned to normal. He found a grim satisfaction in that even as he knew what his brother would think of it.

At the far side of the house, closest to the road, he found the telephone line. It had been cut. Whoever these guys were, they weren't taking any chances on help being summoned. His hand tightened on the gun.

He started forward again. About ten yards ahead, a bush moved. He went down fast. There was no sound, but the air directly to the right of his head vibrated as the bullet tore through it.

Silencer. His eyes narrowed. Low to the ground, head pressed to the earth, he heard movement. The man who had fired at him was coming closer, probably to see what effect he'd had. Riordan rolled to his side, came up slightly, and waited, not breathing.

Closer, closer, one more step, another. Riordan could

hear him now, panting slightly, the bushes rustling around him. He'd think he had all the advantages, could take his time picking off anyone he had to. Riordan pressed against the house, the stone warm on his back. The shadows swallowed him.

The man passed him less than an arm's length away. Riordan saw him clearly. A big man, tall and lean, with hard features, sallow skin, neatly trimmed blond hair. A flash of sun touched his white collar.

Riordan tasted bile in his mouth. He had broken with the church so long ago that he wouldn't have believed himself capable of feeling such a sense of betrayal, yet it was there all the same.

His mind, struggling to override the sudden and dangerous surge of emotion, catalogued the reasons why the clerical garb was merely expedient. Here even more than in New York, the appearance of a priest would be unquestioned. Few would ever think to suspect a man of the cloth. Even Riordan, shorn of faith as he was, had trouble doing it.

He followed, carefully, staying far enough back not to draw attention as the black-clad figure approached the kitchen. He pushed the door in and followed quickly. Gun at the ready. Riordan was close enough to see him scan the interior, noting the burned food still on the stove and the chairs pushed back from around the table.

Softly, under his breath, the man called, "Ricci?"

There was no response. The man moved on. Riordan waited a moment before following. The living area was also deserted as was the entry hall. The door to the library opened. Jocelyn stood framed in it. She was white-faced, even her lips seemed bloodless. Behind her, visible over her shoulder, was the second man.

He was also tall and slender with close-cropped dark hair and deep-set eyes that even at a distance held a deadly gleam. The gun he held was an automatic with silencer. He looked pleased to be where he was, doing what he was doing. "Anything?" he asked.

The first man shook his head. "You?"

"Most definitely. Come and see."

The first man disappeared into the library. The door closed behind him.

Riordan waited a full minute before backing away. He went out through the kitchen, intending to find Brendan and tell him what he had learned. But there was no sign of his brother. Sir David, however, was another matter. Riordan found him near the cottage, well concealed by it but with a good view of the library.

His host nodded when he saw him. Together, they knelt near the bushes and looked toward the house.

"I should have gotten the women out," Sir David said, "but I wasn't absolutely sure what we were dealing with."

"Two men," Riordan said, "both priests, one named Ricci who seems to be in charge. They're in the library now."

"Weapons?"

"Automatics with silencers. The blond fired at me."

They exchanged a hard look. There was more at stake than the scroll. A great deal more.

"I caught a glimpse of them," Sir David said. "Am I correct in thinking they really are priests?"

"They sure look like it."

"Could be disguises."

"I don't think so. My guess is Brendan recognized them. Any idea where he is?"

"He went round the other side to take a look from there."

"We can't wait much longer. You know they didn't come just for the scroll?"

Sir David nodded. "The silencers are rather a give-away. Nasty business, this."

"Very," Riordan said grimly. "Two entrances to the library?"

"That's right. One from the inside and the other through the garden directly in front of us. I suggest the latter, of course."

Of course, Riordan thought. The field of fire was far better, especially with them both shooting.

Sir David checked his weapon. He looked up from it into Riordan's eyes. "By the way, how good a shot are you?"

"Sharpshooter or better. You?"

"I've kept up. All right then, let's go. I'll take the left. Pen will know to keep clear of the windows. She and Jocelyn should be toward the back of the room. The table is in the center."

Riordan nodded. He remembered well enough. They moved quickly, going in opposite directions at first to avoid the most direct sight lines from the library. Out of the corner of his eye, he saw Sir David, moving low and fast. Had his wife not been involved, he might even have been enjoying himself.

They reached the outside wall of the house at the same time and closed in on the library door. Sounds reached them from inside. Riordan recognized Ricci's voice. He was speaking calmly, without apparent emotion, but his words were chilling.

"Fornicator. Whore. You have had carnal knowledge of

a man not your husband. You have conspired with a heretic and a nonbeliever to rob the church of its true property. You have sought to act against us, to sway the weak-minded, to widen the door by which evil enters the world. And you dare, you have the audacity, to remonstrate with me for doing what is necessary to protect all that is good and pure and holy?"

There was the sound of a blow. Riordan stiffened and started forward. A gesture from Sir David stopped him. The older man mouthed a single word: Wait.

"This must stop at once." It was Lady Penelope's voice. "You are a priest. You cannot behave like this."

"Keep silent. Women are not to speak before God and certainly not to give direction to man. Not even English women."

"I'm American," Jocelyn said. She spoke with some difficulty. The blow had caught her across the mouth. Her lower lip was bleeding but she didn't care about that. She was too angry to care about much of anything except this inflated caricature standing in front of her, waving his gun in her face, and spouting insane doctrine.

"I'll say anything I want. You're nuts. You come in here, threaten us, and for what? For some phony artifact that's not worth anything. If you're actually priests, the church is in even worse trouble than I thought."

Riordan grimaced. He knew what she was trying to do, to convince Ricci and the other one that they believed the scroll was a fake so that they would be content to simply take it and leave. It was a gamble with small chance of success but at the moment it was all she had.

He moved his head slightly, just enough to see into the room. Jocelyn was sitting on the couch at the back, holding a hand to her face. Lady Penelope was beside her.

Ricci stood in front of them, the gun in his right hand. In his left he held the ivory and gold cylinder. The other man, the blond, was over at the table. He had Riordan's notes in his hand.

"They were translating it, Monsignor," he said. "They know the contents."

"We know it's a fake," Jocelyn insisted. "We were already planning to return it. There is no reason for you to concern yourselves. Surely you know that Wilbur Holcroft would never permit us to sell such a discredited object."

Ricci smiled, a twisting of his mouth that inspired no confidence. "The redoubtable Mr. Holcroft. He will be well rid of you. Get up."

"What are you talking about? Why would Mr. Holcroft want to be—"

"Silent! The chattering of women is as the screeching of magpies, an assault to the ears and an offense to the spirit."

"Good heavens," Lady Penelope murmured, "you do have a bad case, don't you? Really, this has gone on quite long enough. I refuse to have the peace and security of my home interrupted in such a particularly nasty manner. And I am most assuredly not going anywhere with you. Stay where you are, dear."

For good measure, she took hold of Jocelyn's hand, holding her firmly in place. Her eyes darted toward the library door.

"Get up!" Ricci ordered again. "I will not tolerate such disrespect. Heretics, both of you, but in the presence of the true faith, you will abase yourselves. Believe me, you will beg for forgiveness!"

"Up yours," Lady Penelope said. Jocelyn gaped at her. So did Ricci. The blond man dropped the notes he'd been holding and started forward. He shouldn't have done that. The moment he moved, Riordan fired. The bullet caught him high in the chest, spun him around, and exploded a shower of bone and blood that splattered the opposite wall.

Lady Penelope screamed. Jocelyn dove for the floor, pulling her along. Sir David fired but Ricci was already moving. The shot hit him in the left shoulder. He dropped the cylinder which went rolling across the floor. Ricci raised his pistol, his face contorted with hate. Aiming directly at Lady Penelope, he fired.

The gun went off but the shot was wild. It struck the plaster ceiling, sending a shower of white dust down into the room. Ricci jerked back, a startled look in his eyes. His hand went to his chest. Directly below his collar, a small, neat hole blossomed.

The priest fell, as though from a great distance. He landed facedown on the carpet, his hand within inches of the cylinder. His fingers twitched toward it. His eyes, focused beyond the library door, began to glaze over. Again his hand moved, straining, and was still.

Brendan lowered the gun. He stepped into the room and stood, looking down at the dead priests. His face was blank. All thought, all emotion seemed washed from it.

Sir David stepped forward and took the gun from him. Brendan let it go without resistance. He knelt beside Ricci, crossed himself, and in a low, steady voice began the act of contrition.

21

"**W**hat are you going to do?" Riordan asked. They were sitting in the kitchen. Lady Penelope had fixed tea to which Sir David added a bracer of whiskey. Outside, the light was fading.

The young, stern-faced men who had come at Sir David's summons from the mainland had been and gone, flying in by helicopter and leaving the same way. With them had gone the bodies of Ricci and the other priest whom Brendan identified as the Monsignor's aide. They would be buried properly but with discretion. No unfortunate questions would be asked.

"I'm going back to Rome," Brendan said quietly, "to see Manzini."

Sir David cleared his throat. He sat beside his wife, holding her hand. Their chairs were drawn close together. "Are you sure that's wise?"

Brendan laughed faintly. He was still pale but Riordan was glad to see some light returning to his eyes. "No, I'm not," he said, "but I don't seem to have any choice. Despite the events of today, I'm still a priest."

He took a long sip of his tea and put the cup down. When he spoke, it was a toss-up who he was trying to convince, himself or his listeners.

"Ricci was an aberration, a renegade. He doesn't represent the church—not my church. Manzini has to understand what he set in motion when he trusted him. Maybe it's a lesson we all need. The church faces tremendous challenges. The temptation to turn back to the old ways can be very strong in certain individuals like Ricci. It has to be resisted with all our strength. If it's not—" He broke off, staring at an unseen vision he did not care to share.

Softly, Jocelyn said, "I think you're doing the right thing. This business needs to be settled once and for all."

Riordan nodded. "I agree and that's why I'm going with you." He held up a hand, stopping Brendan before he could object. "Don't trot out all the reasons why I shouldn't. The fact is we're in this together. You say Ricci was an aberration, but I'm not so sure. There may be others like him."

"There's only one way it can be settled," Brendan said softly. "You know that."

The two brothers stared at one another. Slowly, Riordan nodded.

Rome lay washed clean, gleaming beneath the sun. Vatican City swarmed with visitors. They crowded the piazza, trotted through the museums, pushed into the gift stalls, sweating, oblivious, enchanted or not as the chance might be.

Beyond, in the private areas, it was a good deal quieter. Also, Jocelyn thought, cooler. She was wearing one of the linen dresses she'd bought on Sardinia. It was a bit plain for Rome but it was all she had until she could get back to the hotel and recover her luggage. Besides, no one seemed to care.

Certainly not the cardinal who sat behind the vast expanse of his desk, robed in scarlet, gazing at them with a mixture of dismay and disbelief. He was a small man in height but more than made up for that in his girth and his presence. His hair was thin and white, his face round, and his eyes, troubled as they were, shone with gentleness.

"Tragic," he murmured when Brendan concluded his report. "I had no idea Ricci was so—unstable. What a terrible waste."

He exhaled deeply, rose, and looked at them all. "What can I say? I am most profoundly sorry. Surely you understand no one intended anything like this to happen. Ricci was merely told to coordinate the recovery of the scroll with Father Nolan."

He sighed again and shook his head. "What perplexes me most is that there was no reason for any of this. Oh, certainly, we didn't care for the breach in security but that could be dealt with. To go to such insane lengths— One can only wonder at the unordered state of poor Ricci's mind."

He shook his head, his shoulders sagging as though beneath the weight of such folly.

"Of course," Brendan said softly. He was wearing his cassock again, starkly black against the ornateness of the room. Jocelyn looked at it, thinking that on Ricci the blackness had been a warning whereas with Brendan it seemed merely suitable to a man firm in his convictions and willing to defend them with his life.

His life, not others. That made all the difference in the world.

"Our only concern, Eminence," Brendan said, "is that Ricci not have left any legacy, perhaps others—here within the Vatican or elsewhere—who shared his attitudes."

"Oh, I really don't think that's likely. But I will act to remove any possibility." The cardinal's hand, plump and beringed, fell on the object lying on his desk. He lifted it gently. "This will go a long way toward assuring that."

Light caught the gold, melted into it, made the old ivory gleam. Jocelyn lowered her eyes.

"You are doing the right thing, my son," the cardinal said.

"I'm doing the necessary thing," Riordan replied. He looked toward Jocelyn, wondering at the stillness in her. It had been there ever since they left Sardinia, some well of silence and thought he could not penetrate. There was no time to do so now.

"Life has to go on for both Miss Merriman and myself. We want to be able to live without fear that our next step may be our last."

"Always desirable," Manzini murmured. He made no effort to refute the suggestion of fear, to deny that it had any legitimacy. That was not his function, not here, in this place and time, at this moment when truth and lies clashed so resoundingly.

"There's just one thing, Eminence," Riordan went on. "I'm doing this on my own terms, not yours. My brother and I don't see eye to eye on much but there's one thing we agree on, neither of us likes being used. You used Brendan, a good, decent, honorable man, and you did it to the point where he had no choice but to kill. There's a price for that. You want to keep the scroll, you tell my brother the truth."

"I see," Manzini said slowly. "Exactly which truth is that? There are a good many in this world, most of them contradictory."

"Not in this case. You told him the scroll was a forgery, a fourth-century fake fabricated in order to harm the church. But that's not the case, is it?" He leaned forward slightly, facing the cardinal who stood, red-robed and flushed. "Truth, Eminence, that's the price. Brendan deserves to know what he killed for."

Manzini smiled. He put a hand to his chest, wheezing softly. "I thought you were a nonbeliever, Professor, yet you show a positively religious attachment to this notion of truth. Very well then." He drew himself up, hands folded. The light fractured within the gems of his rings and set to dancing.

"Father Nolan," he said formally, as befitted the occasion. "I owe you a particular apology. When I delegated this matter to you, I repeated certain assertions about the scroll which have always been Vatican policy but which in fact I knew to be false. Indeed, had your mind not been clouded by all that has occurred, you most likely would have realized that for yourself." Softly, he said, "If the scroll had merely been a dangerous forgery, we would have destroyed it long ago."

Brendan stared at him. He was not surprised, as much as he longed to be. There was only sadness in him, that and determination. So his brother had been right. What else had he been correct about? Later, perhaps, he would think about that. But for now—

"You're saying it really is the testament of Mary Magdalen?"

Manzini nodded. "So we believe."

"Which makes it even more dangerous, doesn't it?" Jocelyn asked. "There's the inference, at least, that Mary may have been a disciple of Christ's, not to mention the statement attributed to Yeshua that suggests a priesthood in authority over lay people isn't necessary or even perhaps desirable. Given all that, why didn't the church destroy it anyway?"

"Because it is what it is," the cardinal said. "We simply would not do that. Just so there is no possibility of misunderstanding—" He turned back to Brendan and handed him the cylinder. "Would you be so kind?"

Brendan's hand closed on one of the turtledove end caps. Slowly, he twisted it open. His face was pale but resolute. He eased the scroll out and unwound the first few inches.

"I'm sure my brother will have no regrets," he said as he rewound the fabric and slid it gently back into the cylinder. His eyes met Riordan's. "As you have said, Eminence, he is doing the right thing."

The cardinal nodded. He took the cylinder back and placed it in the center of his desk. His hand shook slightly. "Well, then, that's done." He smiled. "Tell me, Miss Merriman, will you be going back to Holcroft & Farnsworth?"

Jocelyn shook her head. "I don't think so. I'm due for a change."

"Ah, yes, under the circumstances, you may be right. And you, Professor, what are your plans?"

"I've been thinking about taking a sabbatical when this term is over," Riordan said. "If you stay in the classroom too long, you risk getting stale."

The cardinal nodded. "Yes, that's true of administrative

duties as well. We tend to lose the sense of what's really important. I would like to invite you to stay for dinner."

"I'm sorry," Riordan said quietly, "we have a plane to catch. However, you'll be staying, won't you, Brendan?"

His brother stood, dark against the crimson walls. He looked tired but resolute. "Yes," he said, "I'll be staying."

Air Italia Flight 902 lifted off from the Rome airport three hours later, climbed to thirty thousand feet, and banked westward on the direct heading to New York.

The cabin attendant poured champagne, inquired about the selections for dinner, and departed. Jocelyn snuggled down into her seat. "I'm wrecked. If I don't move for a week, it'll be too soon."

"Same here," Riordan said. He shifted slightly and groaned. "I told you I wasn't as young as I used to be but would you listen? Oh, no. Tear me out of my nice, safe little office, away from my nice, safe little classes, send me crawling through catacombs, getting shot at, shooting back no less which I haven't done in years and never planned on doing again. It's enough to give a person a complex."

"You loved it," Jocelyn said. "Besides, it brought you closer to your brother."

Riordan sighed. "Oh, yes, I'm sure Brendan sees it that way. He starts out lying to me, ends up having to kill a fellow priest, and finally has to accept the fact that a good deal of what he's based his life on may be on a very shaky foundation."

"Is it?" Jocelyn asked. She reached out, touching his arm lightly, feeling the strength and warmth that radiated from him. "Not if Brendan is anything to go by. He came through splendidly. You should be proud of your brother."

"I am," Riordan admitted. "He surprised me in the end."

"Because you thought he wouldn't do what was needed?"

"I suppose not. We haven't agreed on anything in so long, I never thought he'd see his way to help us keep the scroll out of the Vatican's hands."

"But he did," Jocelyn said, "even though it meant yet more lies. He convinced Manzini that strip of linen with your scribbling on it was genuine. No mean feat, that."

Riordan's eyebrows rose. "Scribbling? I'll have you know I labored a full day and night to copy that much of the scroll. It was all I had time for and if anyone other than Brendan had opened it, we would have been cooked. Which, by the way, raises a question. Why didn't Manzini check it for himself?"

"Why do you think?"

"Because he's gotten in the habit of having other people do things for him, even important things like that? Because he wanted to show my brother he still trusted him even after Brendan killed Ricci? Because he was trying to make amends in his own fashion?"

"Maybe," Jocelyn said. She sounded unconvinced. "I've got another question for you. What was that you meant when you reminded me that not all the Khalduns had been killed? Surely you aren't thinking that—"

"Wild, isn't it? More than nine hundred years after the scroll is taken from them, somebody breaks into the Vatican archives and takes it back. It's stretching credulity to think that happened by accident."

"You think Saleem . . . ?"

"May have a very interesting family tree, all the way back to that one Khaldun son di Costello said survived."

"Then why try to sell the scroll?" Jocelyn asked. "Why not just keep it?"

"I'm not convinced he was going to sell it. I think he wanted authentication and publication—to get the truth out. But he also wanted to keep some distance between himself and the inevitable fallout. So he enlisted your help."

"You realize this is all speculation," Jocelyn said quietly.

Riordan nodded. "We may never really know what happened but I'm sure of one thing—"

His face brightened, filled with excitement and expectation. "There's more of it, Jocelyn. I'm sure of that. We can find it."

We. She'd let that go by for the moment. First, she asked, "How do you plan to do that?"

"First, I'm going to wrap up my classes and finish work on the part we've got. When the term is over, I'm going to Surrey to talk to Jamal. I'm convinced he knows something about the Khalduns that he hasn't told. Depending on what he says, the next stop is Jerusalem. Granted the trail is centuries cold, but if there's any trace of them left, that's where it will be. Then there's Beirut. Conditions are a lot better there. We can check out Hassan, see where that goes. And then—"

"What about the di Costellos?" Jocelyn asked.

Riordan frowned. "What about them?"

"They were old acquaintances, if not friends, of the Khalduns. Lorenzo claimed to have saved the eldest son's life. Maybe he got something for it. We might find out that he brought home some interesting souvenirs from his trip to the Holy Land."

"I doubt the family still exists," Riordan said but his

mind was already working, imagining how whatever remnants remained could be tracked down. "Brendan might be able to help with that."

"I don't think you want to involve him with it," Jocelyn said. "At least not right away."

"Why not?"

She smiled and shook her head. "Here's dinner. I'm starved."

So was Riordan, sufficiently to be distracted. Flight 902 flew on, racing the night. The movie was a new James Bond adventure, filled with international intrigue and derring-do. It held no interest for them. Presently, they slept.

The cabin attendant, passing their seats, paused to switch off the lights and cover them both with blankets. He noted as he did so that the woman still held her carry-on bag on her lap, clutching it as she might a precious child.

22

It was hot in New York. Not the weak, wimpy heat that infects the city from time to time, but the dead down, no holds barred, tropical rain forest heat that comes complete with 99.99 percent humidity, temperature inversion, and enough glare to smelt steel.

Hot.

But then it was July and that sort of thing had to be expected.

Jocelyn poured herself yet another glass of iced spearmint tea. She was making it herself these days but still hadn't quite perfected Trey's technique. She would eventually, it was just a matter of letting it steep long enough, or maybe the freshness of the spearmint leaves, or the water—

She could call him and ask but they'd all been so busy over at Holcroft & Farnsworth ever since Wilbur's heart attack that Trey probably wouldn't have time to talk. Wilbur was gone, hustled off to some nursing home in Connecticut, and there was a grand shuffle underway to reapportion the various fiefdoms. Incredible as it sounded, Trey had a good shot at antiquities. After all, he knew the right people.

Jocelyn wished him well. She wouldn't have traded places with him for the world. Actually, she couldn't have. Riordan would have objected.

They were hanging around her apartment, lacking the energy to go anywhere, with the air conditioner going, the refrigerator stocked, and a weekend's worth of videos waiting to be watched. They'd wait for a while.

She heard a sound from the bedroom and turned toward it. Riordan stood at the door, rumpled, smiling, and gorgeously nude. He yawned and scratched his chest.

"Got anything to eat?"

"That's what I love about you. You're such a romantic."

"That's it? I thought it was something else. A few minutes ago, you said—"

To her astonishment, Jocelyn felt herself blush. She wouldn't have thought she could still do that, all things considered.

"Never mind. How about a turkey sandwich?"

"With Russian dressing, shredded lettuce, and tomato, on a roll?"

"Sure, why not?"

He grinned and sat down at the counter. "You spoil me."

"Boy, do I ever. By the way, my mother called."

Riordan put on his brave look. "That's nice. What did she want?"

"She wants us to come to dinner Friday night."

"Can we do that?"

"I don't see why not. Besides, if we don't, I'll never hear the end of it. They're crazy about you."

Her whole family was, down to her kid sister who told Riordan he was a hunk and brought her girl friends around to meet him, her brother-in-law who it turned out had been in Vietnam at about the same time as Riordan and thought their paths had crossed somewhere in the Mekong Delta, her father who made no secret of his infinite relief that his daughter had not wed a limp-wristed, turned-up-collar preppie who wouldn't know how to go about getting a man his grandchildren if his life depended on it and, last but not least, Jocelyn's mother who cooed over Riordan disgracefully, plied him with brisket and allowed as to how she'd always known there was someone in Jocelyn's past the poor girl was pining for and, thank God, it had all worked out in the end.

Just another Friday night in the Mulkowsky household. When they actually got married next week, the family would really get rolling.

"Relax," Riordan said. "They'll settle down."

"When?"

"Fifty years or so, they'll get used to me. Some of the glamour and charisma will wear off. Not much, mind you, but some. They'll forget how incredibly relieved they were, and grateful really that I came along to take you off —Ouch! That hurt."

"It was supposed to. For an out-of-work college professor, you talk a pretty good line."

"So do you, for an out-of-work antiquities curator. Has it occurred to you that neither of us has a job?"

"Uh-uh, not true. Sir David called."

Riordan rolled his eyes. "Do I want to hear this?"

"It's a little thing, he said, nothing major, a matter of dropping something off in Jerusalem when we're there next month. He said he'd explain more when we see him in London."

"What happened to Sardinia?"

"I'm not sure. Lady Pen said something vague about old war horses but she sounded happy."

She finished putting the sandwich together and set it in front of him. A lock of hair was falling into his eyes. She brushed it aside gently.

Riordan caught her hand, turned it over, and pressed his mouth lightly to her palm. The tremor that ran through her was deep and lasting. Beneath the cotton man's shirt she wore, her nipples hardened.

"We have work to do," she said.

He groaned. "Don't remind me."

They had spent the previous week packing up his apartment. Jocelyn still had trouble believing some of the things he'd had squirreled away in there, boxes of pottery shards, bits and pieces of figurines waiting to be reassembled, old coins worn so smooth as to be almost indecipherable, all the flotsam and jetsam of vanished civilizations that few considered of any importance but which Riordan saw as clues to the vast design of humanity.

He had refused to part with anything, necessitating umpteen trips to the local liquor store and grocery to beg boxes. By comparison, her place would be a snap. She glanced around without regret, already seeing the walls bare, the furniture removed, her life disassembled.

"What are you thinking about?" Riordan asked.

"That's it's funny how hard I worked to get where I was and how easily I let it go in the end."

"You don't have to," he said quietly, "at least not entirely. Plenty of auction houses would be glad to get you. We could work it out."

"Maybe, but then you'd be running all over having fun and I'd be stuck in an office. No thanks. I'd rather wing it."

He grinned. "Know something, you've changed."

"So have you. What happened to being scared of commitment?"

"I found something more frightening."

"What's that?"

"Being without you."

"I said it before, I'll say it again, you're good." But she was pleased all the same and her face showed it.

Riordan laughed. He reached out for her, the sandwich forgotten.

He remembered it again an hour or so later, and did justice to it. They got down to work finally, filling the boxes piled up in the living room. The day faded and evening was creeping up over the city before they were done.

Riordan snapped the tape over the last box and carried it over to the others. "Want to go out tonight?" he asked.

"Sure, might as well." She grimaced. "I've got to get cleaned up first."

She got into the shower, he followed, one thing led to another. They had dinner late. Returning to the apartment, Riordan yawned. In bed, they nestled together, seeking the already familiar arrangement of arms and legs. It was their last night in the apartment. Tomorrow, everything went into storage and they headed for London, then Surrey and whatever else might come.

But first—

Riordan woke in the night. The door to the bedroom

was closed. Only a sliver of light shone under it. He got up, padded across the room, and opened the door.

Jocelyn was sitting cross-legged on the floor. The scroll was in front of her, unrolled to its full length. Gently, she brushed her finger over the surface, lingering in several places.

"What are you doing?" Riordan asked.

Her head lifted. Her eyes were smoky and dark, different from any way he had seen them before. Her hair drifted around her, casting her features into shadow. When she spoke, her voice was husky.

"Putting the pieces together."

"I thought we'd already done that?"

She shrugged and turned back to the scroll. "Why didn't Manzini check it himself?"

Riordan frowned. It was the same question she'd asked on the plane coming home. But now he sensed there was an answer he'd missed.

She laughed softly. "You know, that more than anything else gives me hope. After everything he'd done—lying to Brendan, sending Ricci after Hassan and then after us, being responsible for the deaths—after all that he at least had the decency not to touch the scroll." She sighed. "Or maybe he was just afraid."

"Afraid of what?" Riordan asked. He took a step farther into the room but stopped there. There was something about her, the protective crouch of her body over the scroll, the sense of stillness he'd felt before, the wonder—

"What?" he asked again.

"This," she said quietly. "He thought we'd returned the real scroll and he wouldn't touch it. He let Brendan do that instead. Hassan broke the seal on the turtledove. Before that, the cylinder lay all those centuries untouched for the same reason Manzini wouldn't handle it."

"What reason?" Riordan asked. He did come closer then, kneeling beside her, worried. "Jocelyn, what are you talking about?"

She smiled faintly. "You're a good man, Riordan, and a brilliant one in many ways but your brother is right about one thing, sometimes it really is a matter of faith. You got all the pieces except one. Manzini told Brendan that if it had only been a dangerous forgery, they would have destroyed it long ago. Why didn't they destroy it anyway? Its being real only made it more dangerous."

"Because of what it is," he said. "The church didn't want to be responsible for destroying an actual artifact." Even as he spoke the words, his expression was changing. So much had been destroyed—accidentally, systematically, wantonly. So much of history had been altered, hidden, denied. When had the church—or any other body of men for that matter—ever shown such respect for the past, especially when their own survival could be at stake.

"I don't know," he said slowly, "why didn't they destroy it?"

Jocelyn took his hand. She laid it gently on the scroll, tracing the warp and weave of the fabric, and the faint rust-colored stains that overlaid it in places.

"Mary was the first one at the tomb to find the stone rolled back. She was the first to realize that the body was gone. To do that, she would have had to go inside. What do you suppose she found there?"

Riordan stared fixedly at the scroll, the delicate fabric covered with spidery writing preserved against all odds down through the centuries of upheaval and controversy.

"*That's* why they didn't destroy it," Jocelyn said quietly. "What you feel right there beneath your hand. Di Costello called it the holiest of holy. Mary knew it would be seen that way. No matter how bad things became, the words she wrote on it—his words—would always be kept safe even by people who might want to reject them."

"You can't be sure of this," Riordan protested. But his voice shook and whatever else he meant to say remained unspoken, forgotten before the overwhelming possibility crashing through his mind.

He had never understood how she managed to write on the linen, how the ink fixed, how it lasted all through the centuries. He had managed to duplicate the effect with great difficulty and only because he used an ink vastly more sophisticated than anything Mary would have had access to. And even then he had no illusions, his efforts would not endure more than a few decades before they faded away.

But hers had not.

"You can't be sure," he repeated.

"I don't need to be. There s more of it, Riordan, probably a lot more. There's so much she doesn't say here, how she met Yeshua, whether he actually called her to follow him as he did Peter and the others, what else she heard him say and, above all, what she saw when she stepped inside that tomb."

"It could all have been destroyed long ago," he protested even as some deep, hidden part of himself rejected that.

"Maybe," Jocelyn agreed, "but I doubt it. The pieces were scattered, certainly, but not destroyed. They're still out there somewhere, waiting to be put back together, to be understood."

Her face was serene as she gently refolded the scroll.

She looked up at him and smiled. "It's late. We've got a lot to do tomorrow."

He nodded, staring at her with the sense growing in him that he had never really seen her before, not truly as she was, seen past the skin and sinew, the bone and blood to deep inside where a small, bright light shone steadily.

He held out his hand. Jocelyn took it. They stood safe within each other's arms.

Far out over the river, a sea bird called. The gray softness of dawn crept out of the east.